Come Home, Nurse Jenny

COME HOME, NURSE JENNY

Colleen L. Reece

Thorndike Press • Chivers Press
Thorndike, Maine USA   Bath, England

Copyright © 1978 by Colleen L. Reece

All rights reserved.

This Large Print edition is published by Thorndike Press, USA and by Chivers Press, England.

Published in 2000 in the U.S. by arrangement with Colleen L. Reece

Published in 2000 in the U.K. by arrangement with Colleen L. Reece.

U.S. Hardcover 0-7862-2580-7   (Candlelight Collection Edition)
U.K. Hardcover 0-7540-4194-8   (Chivers Large Print)

The text of this Large Print edition is unabridged.
Other aspects of the book may vary from the original edition.

Set in 16 pt. Plantin.

Printed in the United States on permanent paper.

British Library Cataloguing in Publication Data available

Library of Congress Cataloging-in-Publication Data

Reece, Colleen L.
     Come home, Nurse Jenny / Colleen L. Reece.
          p.   cm.
     ISBN 0-7862-2580-7 (lg. print : hc : alk. paper)
     1. Nurses — Fiction. 2. Large type books. I. Title.
PS3568.E3646 C66   2000
813′.54—dc21
                                              00-028681

Come Home, Nurse Jenny

Chapter 1

The hospital-staff dining room was crowded. It seemed everyone had come in for lunch at the same time on this particular day. Dr. Lance Reeves raised his voice in order to be heard above the din. With a bitter twist to his mouth he glanced pointedly at the chattering group of nurses nearby. His voice was full of scorn, lashing the words into an unpleasantness that shocked even his fellow doctors, who knew their young colleague well.

"Look at them! A giggling bunch of maidenhood! And they are to be the ones to help humanity! What a laugh. Most of them will either marry and quit now that their training is finished or else get a high-paying job in some doctor's office! There's probably not one in the entire bunch who knows the meaning of those caps they wear so cockily!"

It was unfortunate that just as he spoke, a little lull had settled over the room. His words, cutting and cold, were heard distinctly by the group of nurses he had scorned. For a moment there was silence; you could almost see the frosty fingers of disdain that swept through the group of young women who were at the end of four long, hard years of training and who would, in only a few days, receive their diplomas and their degrees. Then a small, shining-brown-haired nurse rose to her feet and determinedly made her way to the table where Dr. Reeves sat with his colleagues. Her cheeks were wearing battle flags of red, and her usually dreamy, large brown eyes were shooting unaccustomed sparks. Those doctors at the table who had worked with Nurse Jennet Trevor, better known and loved as "Jenny" throughout the hospital, had never seen her like this.

She paused next to Dr. Reeves, fingers unconsciously lacing together as though for strength. Her voice, clear as a bell, commanded the attention of every person in the dining room when she spoke. "You're wrong, Dr. Reeves."

Her challenge rang out to the man in white, who was cynically listening to what she would say. This was a new experience for him. Nurses didn't challenge doctors; it simply wasn't done. Yet here was this small, determined nurse facing him with fire in her eyes.

"What I said still goes," he informed her. "I don't think I've had the" — he looked her up and down — "the pleasure of meeting you, Miss — ?"

"I'm Jennet Trevor." There was a lilt in her voice that should have warned the doctor here was no weak opponent, in spite of her demure appearance. She rushed on, words tumbling over each other.

"You seem to be quite scornful of our class." She cocked her head at the group she had left, unaware of their frozen silence. This couldn't be happening, not their Jenny! Didn't she know she could be reprimanded severely? In spite of being head of her class, she could even yet be denied graduation if she was charged with insubordination and rudeness to a doctor, but nothing stopped her.

"I will not allow you or any doctor to challenge my right to my cap," she told the doctor. "You say we will either marry and quit or go into a high-paying job. That is ridiculous! Three of our class have already signed with the Peace Corps. Two more are slated for work in Appalachia, where their skill is needed tremendously. Several others have asked for positions of every kind throughout this country. And you, you" — her voice increased in its fury —

"you have the gall to sit there in judgment on us, a 'giggling bunch of maidenhood.' " She paused for breath.

The doctor, stung more than he would admit, inserted, "And you, Miss Trevor? I notice you carefully left yourself off that list of idealistic occupations. What will you do with your skills?" The words were biting. They would have shriveled a less upset nurse.

The waiting crowd held its collective breath for her answer. There was something grand about this nurse who had upheld her fellow classmates. What would she say in her own defense? It came simply.

"I am going home."

"Home?" the doctor barked. "Some little dump where you can marry your childhood sweetheart and kid yourself into thinking you are helping humanity? You are going home, Miss Trevor?" His words brought tears of sheer anger to the lovely brown eyes turned on him.

"Yes, Lancelot . . ."

"Lancelot!"

Jenny swallowed hard. Now she had done it. Evidently Dr. Lance Reeves had heard the nickname she had dubbed him with when he first came to the hospital, due to his clean good looks and dark blue eyes. The touch of premature silver at the temples of his black hair only increased his attractiveness. He would have been charming if he had not been so cynical.

"Yes! Lancelot!" The chin was lifted higher as Jenny continued to look into the doctor's challenging eyes, even when he stood to his feet at her words.

"You prate of service to humanity! Just what are you doing with your skill as a surgeon?" She motioned to his left arm, lying still in its carefully held position against his side. Words poured out that she would have kept back, if she could. She seemed to have lost control, and none of those in the dining room would ever have spoken to the doctor as she did then.

"For four years I have studied so I would have knowledge to help those who really needed it. Did you ever hear of Lake Chelan and a little valley called Stehekin at the head of it? A place accessible only by water or air? That's where I'm going, Dr. Lancelot Reeves! Would you like to hear how hard the people there have tried to interest a doctor in coming to their area? The only medical help they have is from a retired doctor who really needs the rest. Shall I tell you how my own sister Twilight

11

lost her baby because that retired doctor was out on another emergency call and they couldn't get her out for help soon enough? Shall I tell you how they have banded together and scrimped and saved, and finally built a little clinic in hopes that some doctor would turn his back on wealth in favor of their need? Or shall I tell you that my going will mean the difference between life and death for some there? Would you like to hear how boat tourists get sick and have no one to care for them? That's home, Dr. Lancelot Reeves. That is where I am going!"

In spite of his discomfort at the situation, the doctor could not help but admire this young woman's spunk. He thought modern women were generally spineless, but this one had the courage of her convictions, and down inside him, a sneaking admiration for her began to grow. There was no sign of it, however, as he retorted, "Do go on, Nurse, do go on!"

There was no mistaking the bite in his words, but Jenny was too angry to care. Very seldom did she lose her temper, but when she did she was apt to do it thoroughly. Without counting the cost, she pounced on the very thing that would most make the man before her squirm.

"You talk of devotion to duty. Then why aren't you doing something with your talents other than teaching in this hospital? Why aren't you using the God-given skills you possess?" There was a slight start in the group as she heedlessly rushed on.

Motioning to the carefully held left arm, she said, "Oh yes, we all know you came back from training army recruits with a badly shattered left wrist, the wrist on your surgeon's hand. So what?" She ignored the pain that swept into his face.

"Why don't you train your right hand to take its place? If I had your skill, nothing would keep me from using it, nothing!"

"That's enough, Jenny!" It was the director of the nursing school who spoke. Her voice was even as she approached the table.

"Let her go on," Dr. Reeves said hoarsely, face white. The nursing director stopped short. She probably couldn't have stopped Jenny at that moment anyway.

"Places like Stehekin are crying for medical help. Small towns everywhere would welcome you as their doctor, with or without your surgical skill. In some place like that, you could help with every facet of medicine and give that wrist a chance to heal. But instead, here you are, teaching dull classes in anatomy while people are dying because of lack of medical attention!" Now there were real tears on her face, tears of earnestness.

"Lancelot followed his dream even though it meant personal sacrifice. Why can't you do the same?" Never had the dining room been so still.

This time when the nursing director spoke, her tones were solid ice. "That will do, Jenny. I will see you in my office in one hour. Now I suggest you return to your duty station . . . immediately."

Her words had the effect of bringing Jenny back to reality. She had been fighting against complacence, lack of caring for those who really needed help. Now she suddenly realized for the first time what she had done. This doctor could demand her dismissal. Four years of work down the drain! What had she done? She seemed to shrink into herself, growing inches smaller as she hesitantly backed away, eyes still on Dr. Reeves, and left the room.

For a moment there was still silence, then Dr. Reeves told the nursing director, "I do not want Miss Trevor reprimanded in any way." He raised his hand to her involuntary protest.

"What she did was highly irregular, but

she had great provocation. She will need that spirit when she goes to wherever she is going — what did she say it was called? Stehekin?" For a space of a heartbeat there was wistfulness in his eyes, quickly replaced with stern admonishment. "Remember, she is not to be censured."

Although the nursing director only replied, "It shall be as you say, Doctor," inside she was rejoicing. What if such a nurse as Jenny had been dismissed, and so close to graduation! She inwardly quailed at the thought.

In the four years she had known the girl, watching her grow into a young woman and an outstanding nurse, she had come to care a great deal for her and to respect her desire to return to her sister's home in that isolated place so far from civilization. Jenny had shared her dreams with the older woman, how she would do what she could as a nurse in the tiny clinic that had been built by the community, keeping in close touch with the doctors in Chelan regarding any treatment, so she might not overstep the bounds of authority of her profession. The nursing director even envied the girl her youth and ideals. Long ago . . .

Brushing the thoughts away, she hurried

to her office. Close on her heels came Dr. Reeves.

"Why did she call me Lancelot?" he demanded when the door closed behind them, shutting out curious eyes. "Is she the one who started it?"

The nursing director shook her head, eyes twinkling. "I believe her roommate Ann Trevor actually used it first. It is a compliment, I assure you. The girls, romantic as they are, saw beyond your good looks a desire to make the world a better place."

Rich red color mantled the doctor's brow, making him a little more human than the icy machine who had faced Jenny. "I used to have ideals — before this." The anguish in his voice as he raised his almost useless left hand reached the woman as nothing else could have done.

She carefully concealed the quick tears that sprang to her eyes and kept her voice matter-of-fact. "Perhaps Jenny is right. Perhaps if you got away into a quiet place . . ." She left the sentence unfinished.

For a long while, Dr. Reeves stared at her. When he spoke again, he seemed to be asking an irrelevant question. "You said her roommate's name was also Trevor?" It served to turn the tide of emotion that had threatened to overflow into the room.

"Yes, we assign the girls alphabetically as roommates. Ann and Jenny have lived together for four years. Seldom have I seen such a team. Ann is really a live wire, bouncy, red-haired, tall, glamorous, but devoted to her profession. Jenny is quiet —" She was interrupted by the doctor's hearty laugh. That was the first time she had ever heard it, she thought reflectively.

"Quiet? I find that a little hard to believe, after today."

The woman across the big desk stuck to her guns. "Usually she is quite reserved. The year before she joined us for training, she underwent open-heart surgery. It gave her an opportunity to realize just how wonderful life is and how much worth living. There is a maturity about Jennet Trevor that is rare for one her age. She will do whatever she attempts to do."

"She has a worthy champion."

"I wish every class brought me a dozen Jennet Trevors! She told me once that sometimes when she first came here she would be homesick for Stehekin. She heard voices in the night calling, 'Come home, Nurse Jenny,' and it was all she could do not to follow them. Then she remembered how she had a talent to

17

develop, a skill to increase. She has done it beautifully and graduates number one in her class."

"Was she born in this Stehekin?"

"No. Her sister went there about five years ago and became teacher in the one-room school when her aunt had an accident. Jenny fell in love with the place the following spring and summer she spent there. She has been back only two or three times, but each time it is a wrench to leave it. Someday I am going to see Stehekin. I want to know what kind of magic a place can hold to call back a talented girl like Jenny when the world would open up before her in her chosen field! She remains true to her dream of helping in that tiny spot carved out of the forests. That's why I cherish her so much."

A hesitant rap on the door effectively stopped their conversation. Answering the director's call to come in, Dr. Reeves's brown-eyed opponent entered, but she was a different girl from the one who had faced him in the dining room. Her face was devoid of color; only the lipstick she wore relieved its paleness. The brown eyes were enormous.

"Oh!" She hadn't expected the doctor to be there. It was evident in the little involuntary gasp she made when she first saw him.

With quick determination, the doctor made a decision. "Would you allow me to handle this?" he courteously asked the director.

She hesitated a moment; it was certainly not the regular way to do things, and yet — "Of course." She rose gracefully and left the room, but not before Lance had seen the half-hidden V for victory she had made to the waiting nurse.

"Won't you be seated, Nurse?" The studied casualness of his voice left Jenny with the feeling of a Christian slave before a Roman emperor, but she didn't betray her feelings as she took the indicated chair.

His first words totally disarmed her. "Tell me about Stehekin."

She stared in amazement. It was the last thing she had expected from this self-contained doctor, about whom there was so much hospital speculation.

Eyes glowing, she leaned forward. Tell about Stehekin? Her voice flowed, pouring out a river of information.

It was a pleasure just to listen to the sound of her voice; it was so soft and strong at the same time. Like silk, the tired doctor thought, leaning back in the chair and half closing his eyes. And her story! It was incredible. Through her words he caught sight of tall mountains, rushing mountain streams, grassy pastures, mountain flowers, a way of life adapted to the wilderness. He had always meant to go to that region, to Cascades National Park and across the new Cross State Highway, but he hadn't been able to fit it into his schedule since coming to Seattle. Now a long-ago desire, memories of childhood running free through buttercups chasing butterflies, haunted him, bringing back forgotten dreams of quietness.

" 'The way through.' " He repeated Jenny's words slowly. She had told him the meaning of the Indian word *stehekin*. Originally, the word referred to the way through the mountains; now it meant much more than that to Jenny and her sister, Twilight, who had both learned to love the out-of-the-way place. Twilight, what a lovely name! The sister was still living there, married to a forester.

Without warning the doctor looked at Jenny. "Are you engaged?"

Caught off guard, she shook her head vigorously. "No. I'm too busy for that yet." Her honest voice reflected some of the confusion she felt at the way the interview

20

was going. She was totally unprepared for his next question.

"What would you give to bring medical help to your Stehekin?"

The answer was fervent and quick in coming. "Anything!"

"Would you care enough about it to marry me?" The words were left hanging in the air as the girl sprang to her feet.

"Marry you? Marry *you?* You must be out of your mind!"

"Perhaps I am," the quiet man across the desk stated in even tones. "But the offer holds."

She dropped back into the chair as if unable to stand. "But why?" she demanded helplessly. "You've never even seen me before today, before I . . ." Her voice faltered. She looked at him as if he were crazy.

Dr. Reeves's fingers were white as he clenched them together. "Let's just say that your words slashed into my consciousness and showed me what a hypocrite I have been, hiding behind my injury." He bent the stiff fingers as far as they would go. "I would like to do what you suggested, find a small place that could use my services and give this hand a chance to heal. Stehekin sounds perfect."

"But why . . ." She couldn't put into words the proposal he had made.

"Even Stehekin wouldn't want a half-doctor," he explained grimly. "If I went as your husband, they would accept me for what I am. And in time, perhaps, I could regain use of these muscles or, as you said, train my right hand in surgical procedures."

Incredible as it seemed, Jenny's heart leaped within her. What an opportunity for Stehekin, and yes, for Dr. Reeves! Surely in that clean mountain air he would grow well. But to marry him, a complete stranger? Not a stranger, her heart argued. How long have you admired and pitied him, longed for him to become the doctor he once must have been? Even though he hadn't known she existed, Jenny had watched the doctor. He fitted the name Lancelot perfectly, and . . . would he become her knight in shining armor? But to marry him? Even for such a cause?

Into Jenny's mind flashed her sister Twilight's face when she had told Jenny, "We are trying again for a child. This time you will be here, Jenny. This time we won't lose our baby." What a godsend a doctor like Dr. Reeves would be for her — and for others!

Jenny's face was as white as that of the stern man opposite her as she demanded, "You . . . you don't mean for this to be a real marriage?"

His instant crisp reply reassured her as nothing else could have done. "Of course not! You think I'd tie you to a cripple? We will be partners only, doctor and nurse. When my wrist heals, then we can see . . ."

Jenny closed her eyes against the sight of him looking directly into her being. Everything she knew about him vied with her ideals of what marriage should be. Yet how could she say no?

Almost without her own volition the whispered answer came. "Yes. I will marry you."

Chapter 2

The words of the graduation speaker forced themselves into Jenny's consciousness, crowding out the turbulent thoughts that had divided her attention. For a moment she glanced around her fellow group of nurses, each one's face rapt and attentive. Four years of hard work and study. Four years of helping and heartbreak. Four years of service, of training. Now they must separate to take that training to where it was needed. For a moment, tears filled the brown eyes watching her classmates with love. Then the guest speaker's comments roused her.

"I am not going to stand here and tell you the world is just waiting out there for your talents and skills. You already know that. I am going to commission you to fight in the battle of life. Most of you will never fight on a battlefield, yet the fight you are facing is much more important! It will be a fight against poverty, against indifference, against those who do not care or will not discipline themselves to take care of the bodies God has given them. You will heal, teach, and learn. You will love, care, and sometimes be brokenhearted when after all you have done, it is not enough and your patient dies. Yet many times you will be thrilled that because of you a soul returns to earth for a little while longer. Those are the moments you must cling to, that make life worthwhile. Those are the times you must cherish, or you will fail. You will not have strength to stand against the disappointments unless your bright courage is fed from wellsprings of happiness.

"Go then, carrying high the torch that all others who have gone before have carried. Some have given their lives for it. Treat it not lightly, this sacred charge. Go, young women who are part of the hope of the world, and lift where you can, love where you can, and serve wherever you are called, that this world might be a better place because you have lived in it."

Even Jenny's irrepressible roommate, Ann, had tears in her eyes. Then the line of young women was filing forward to receive the long-coveted diplomas, signed and sealed, proclaiming to the world that here were servants qualified to take their place.

When Jenny reached for hers, the director of the nursing school paused.

"Miss Jennet Trevor, whose faithful discharge of duties and high scholarship has earned her the title of summa cum laude, with the greatest honors!"

The applause was deafening. Through the mist that threatened Jenny's vision, she saw her beloved sister Twilight and Twilight's husband, Jefferson Stone, rising to their feet with the rest, in acclamation. She saw Dr. Lance Reeves standing, applauding, with no trace of his usual cynicism.

The look he gave her started color flying like a flag in her cheeks and a feeling of resentment in her usually gentle disposition. What right did he have to look like that, as if he were a mother hen and one of the chicks had done something very great? Just because she had said she would marry him . . . She quickly pushed aside that thought. Time enough to face later the results of her promise.

It was over. The girls had laughed, cried, bidden each other farewell, and exchanged addresses. There was solemnity mixed with joy. Perhaps never again would their group all be together. In time they would lose touch, as classes always do. But not with Ann, Jenny thought.

The tall redhead was already saying to Twilight, "Don't forget, I'm taking the summer off. How soon can I come to Stehekin and still be 'proper'?"

Twilight laughed. It was the same chime of silver bells that characterized Jenny's laughter. The great purple eyes grew brilliant; her face lit up. Only now was she beginning to show signs of approaching motherhood, and it enhanced her natural beauty.

I hope I can look like that when I have children, Jenny thought wistfully. But a moment later the memory of her promise to Dr. Reeves stepped between her and the thoughtful gaze at Twilight. Small chance of that now! What had she done? And what was she to tell Twilight and Jeff, who could see through her like a freshly washed pane of window glass? She needn't have worried.

"Here you are, Jenny!" A muscular arm was slipped around the small waist, a beaming face drew close to her own and kissed her soundly in spite of the audience. When she hurriedly withdrew from the unexpected embrace, Jenny's face was flaming, but not so Dr. Reeves's.

"I'm Lance," he explained. Then at Twilight's puzzled stare, mirrored on Jeff's face, he wrinkled his brow and turned accusingly to Jenny.

"You mean you haven't told them? Jenny, how could you!" There was reproof in his voice, and if it hadn't been for the devilish gleam she alone could see in his eyes, even Jenny would have been taken in by his remarks, they sounded so genuine.

"I . . . I . . ." She faltered, but he went smoothly on.

"I guess I shouldn't blame her too much. She's been so excited over graduation, and then it hasn't been too long since we actually made up our minds to set the date so soon," he drawled, stifling Jenny's protest with a warning pressure on her arm. She bit her tongue to keep from denying what he said, but the memory of her promise was strong. She had been raised always to keep her word, even if it killed her. And this time it very well might, she thought with a sinking heart! Dr. Reeves had certainly taken over the situation. Would he keep his part of the bargain that they would be partners only, or . . . She refused to finish the errant thought. A pulse pounded madly in her forehead, and she realized the brash young doctor was still talking.

". . . decided there was no reason to wait. After all, Stehekin needs medical help, perhaps more than even Jenny can provide. I can certainly use the outdoors and clean air to give this wrist a chance to really heal." He extended his left hand, flexing the muscles a bit. "So, tomorrow, after this young lady becomes Mrs. Doctor Reeves, we're going home with you to Stehekin!"

If Twilight's gasp hadn't been so loud, Jenny's would surely have echoed throughout the room. Tomorrow! She hadn't known it would be so soon.

Smiling as if it were all a huge joke, Dr. Reeves said, "Jenny has told me all about Aunt Lucy's cabin, where you used to live, and about the new home you built. That cabin sounds like just the place for a honeymoon."

Jenny closed her eyes tight. This couldn't be happening, it just couldn't! Honeymoon! The audacity of the man, to stand there and tell all this to her sister and the others — including Ann, whose mouth threatened to permanently dislocate from sheer shock. Even she was effectively silenced by Dr. Reeves's next laughing explanation.

"Miss Ann — I can't call you Miss Trevor just yet, until Jenny becomes Mrs.! But we will certainly welcome you to Stehekin! Of course, you will probably want to stay with Mr. and Mrs. Stone the first visit, since we'll be so newly married, but there will be many visits, I'm sure!"

Ann found herself caught up by the charm of the laughing man before her. Could this be the stone-faced doctor they had known? Stealing a look at Jenny, she couldn't make sense of the odd look on her face. How could she have kept her romance a secret? Perhaps she hadn't. What a dumb idea, Ann thought to herself disgustedly. Yet there was something strange about the whole thing. The announcement, the shock on Twilight and Jeff's faces, the assurance of Dr. Reeves's plans. Wisely, Ann kept silent. Whatever Jenny was doing, she would be convinced it was right. If she chose not to explain, that was her business.

Twilight had finally regained her senses. After all, this was Jenny's big moment. If she had kept it secret, perhaps it was to . . .

"What a wonderful surprise," she said convincingly and, after a pointed glance at the doctor, gathered Jenny close in her arms. "Jenny, you've really pulled a coup. Stehekin will be delighted that you are coming home — and bringing a doctor back with you! And think what it will mean to us, Jeff, with the baby due in late September!" Her eyes were shining now not with mere pride in Jenny's accomplishments, but with anticipation of her own needs. This time there would be no heartbreak with the coming of their child. A real doctor, right there in Stehekin!

Impulsively she turned to Dr. Reeves. "I don't know how to thank you." There was no mistaking the warmth of her voice, nor the sincerity of the kiss she placed on his cheek.

For the first time the good doctor seemed uncertain. Perhaps he hadn't counted on such instant acceptance, Jenny thought wickedly, almost chortling aloud in her pleasure at his discomfiture. Yet her honest heart reproached her. After all, wasn't this the best way? If she had attempted to explain, especially to Ann, perhaps the truth would have been told, and that mustn't happen, she told herself fiercely. If Twilight thought I was marrying in order to provide a doctor for Stehekin and especially for her, she would move heaven and earth to prevent it.

Now was the time for her to speak. "This amazing man of mine." She leaned comfortably against Dr. Reeves's sturdy shoulder. "How like him to make all the plans and then tell me! I didn't know our marriage was to be quite so soon, but as he says, why not?" This was carrying the war right into the enemy camp, but Jenny had burned her bridges. Not for anything would she welsh now.

Ignoring his quizzical look, she demanded, "Just what are our plans, Lance?" She bit off the "Lancelot" she had nearly spoken aloud. No need to antagonize him at this point. If she had thought to catch him unawares, she was disappointed.

"There's a little chapel in a quiet area here in Seattle. I've reserved it for two o'clock tomorrow afternoon."

He turned his charming smile on Twilight and Ann. "Can you help Jenny find a dress tomorrow morning?" He ignored her indignant gasp. "I'm sorry I am rushing you so, darling, but I know you'll want a wedding gown of some kind, and whatever you wear will be beautiful to me."

He certainly was going all out, Jenny thought bitterly. A wedding gown? That was what he expected? All right. She would not only get a wedding gown, she would do some of it her way!

Only a hint of her inner turmoil showed as she answered sweetly, "Oh yes, Lance! And I want gowns for Twilight and Ann also. I can't be married even in a small chapel without them as my attendants!"

Her change of tone didn't even touch him. He smiled. "Of course, dear! And Jeff will be my best man, of course. Do you want to ask some of the others in your class to attend?"

Horrors! What a thought! But Jenny was determined not to let this arrogant creature suspect for one moment that he was getting the best of her. She appeared to reflect for a minute.

"N-no. I think not. They are already set with their own plans. We'll just keep it family." But after a moment, she amended, "Oh yes, I know! Twilight, we must ask Mr. and Mrs. Matthewson, who were so good to us after our parents died, when we lived in their upstairs apartment here in Seattle."

Twilight nodded in full agreement. "Jeff and I will ask them tonight. We're staying there." Her tone became brisk. "What time do the stores open, Jenny? We've got a big job to do before two o'clock tomorrow!"

The radiance of her sister's face as she leaned close and whispered, "I like him!" was all that kept Jenny from crying aloud. A real wedding, white dress, bridesmaids? For the empty marriage theirs would be?

33

What a travesty. How could she go through with it? Then she compared the happy Twilight before her with the grief-stricken one when she lost her first baby and steeled herself.

Whispering a quick prayer, as was her habit since childhood — "Please, God, help me do what I have to do" — she answered, "Nine-thirty. I'll be ready and with bells on!"

In a little while all of the others were gone, and Jenny was in Dr. Reeves's car heading for the nurses' residence, not far away. No longer was he the smiling, debonair man who had carried off so well the deception they were about to enter into. His eyes were keen as he looked at her. "You did quite well, my dear."

Was he laughing at her? It was too much for Jenny. "You realize, of course, that tonight's performance has made me despise you! Talking about Aunt Lucy's cabin and our h-h-honeymoon!" Indignation made her stammer.

This time the doctor definitely did laugh, but when he saw how near to tears Jenny was, he became serious. "Don't make a tragedy of it, Jenny." His voice was kind, almost tender. "I felt this might in the long run make it easier for you. That splendid sister and brother-in-law of yours would suspect if they didn't think we were as ecstatically happy as we ought to be. Can't you play the game? Let the future take care of itself."

Surprisingly enough, his even tones helped Jenny immensely. She mopped up her tears and even smiled at him, a little weakly. "All right." This was the last they spoke before they reached the nurses' residence.

When he took her to the door and she looked up at him in mute appeal, he realized what a strain she had been through. With a murmured, "In case we have an audience . . ." he held her close and kissed her.

Ignoring the storm signals in her eyes, he ran down the steps, turning to call from the bottom, "Good night, Jenny!" He went on to the car, whistling.

Whistling! How could he whistle when everything was such a mess? Jenny shook her head helplessly. Yet his matter-of-fact acceptance of the situation reassured her. After all, if any of the other nurses had been observing their leavetaking, they would surely wonder after they heard of the wedding why the ardent bridegroom hadn't even kissed his fiancee good night the night before the wedding! Luckily her own floor was deserted. Except for Ann and herself, the others wouldn't be staying at the residence that night. They had scattered in all different directions. Jenny crept up the stairs past the first floor, where the underclassmen were evidently holding an impromptu party. Tomorrow they would be moving up to replace the senior students. A rush of emotion filled Jenny as she entered her sparse room one last time. Tomorrow . . .

"I'm glad Ann had a date," she said aloud, meeting her own flushed, tear-stained face in the mirror. "I can pretend to be asleep when she comes in, and tomorrow we'll be too much occupied with the wedding to have a third-degree session!"

The thought of Ann tipped up the corners of her mouth until she was more like herself. No more woebegone creature. After all, tomorrow was another day. Why cross bridges until she came to them? But the hand that pushed her heavy, shining hair back from her forehead trembled at the thought of those future bridges.

One. Two. The clock in the bell tower struck. Jenny was standing at the back of the chapel with Jeff; her brown eyes looked enormous. Jeff touched her hand reassuringly, reminding her of how staunch a friend he had been ever since they first met.

"Your doctor is tops," he whispered. "We went around together this morning for flowers and such, and he is really great! You've picked yourself a winner, Jenny." Her face lit with bright red, but he attributed it to excitement. There was no further time for words. Twilight had insisted Jenny walk down the aisle with Jeff so he could give her away.

The white lace gown was simple, yet effective. Jenny hadn't been able to stand the thought of a veil, so she wore a plain Juliet cap. But the flowers she carried were fantastic! No pristine whiteness for Dr. Reeves! He had not only had the entire front altar decorated with all the colors of early summer roses, but her bouquet was matched to the garlands that draped the little alcove where they were to stand. Crimson Glory, yellow Western Suns, pink Bewitched, all the choice roses, one each, gathered into an old-fashioned paper-lace frill and finished off with baby's breath and tiny blue forget-me-nots. Jenny's eyes had opened wide when she saw them, and Twilight and Ann had been ecstatic.

"I hope someone loves me that much sometime," Ann said enviously. She looked lovely in her pale yellow gown, contrasting with the rich larkspur blue of Twilight's. They had demurred against standing up with Jenny, but she had convinced them that if they didn't she would never be sure it was legal!

For a moment, Jenny felt trapped. She was entering into marriage, something she had been trained to feel was a lifetime endeavor. And for what reason? A great love? She had always felt she would never marry until she knew that only that one person could complete her happiness.

Is it so wrong? she asked herself, as she walked slowly toward the altar. Twilight's face glowed. Jeff approved. Ann had evidently been totally won over by the flowers — and the ring, Jenny reminded herself. Special delivery had brought her a solitaire set in gold; the depth and clarity of the diamond proclaimed it to be rare. A note had accompanied it. "It was my mother's. I hope you like it. If you'd rather have it set differently, we'll attend to that later."

How could he have thought of so many different things? Jenny asked herself. He must have somehow gotten a special license. Of course, because of their professions they already had blood tests on record. She couldn't know how frantically Dr. Reeves had worked from the moment she left the nursing director's office after their fateful interview.

She was at the altar, her small hand being transferred from Jeff's arm to Dr. Reeves's strong, sure one. Afterward she was to be thankful she had listened intently to the wedding service. It was more a service than a mere ceremony. The white-haired, kindly minister dwelled on the relationship of husband and wife, with God as the third party to true marriage. Snatches of it stood out. Her own faltering promise to love, honor, cherish. Her involuntary start of surprise when the minister asked, "Do you, Lancelot Reeves, take this woman . . ."

So his name really was Lancelot! For a moment Jenny's irrepressible sense of humor surfaced from the frozen state in which she was held. She couldn't help but squeeze his hand wickedly as his clear, ringing, "I do!" echoed through the chapel.

There was a biding-my-time look in the glance he gave her when the minister finished the service with, "I pronounce you man and wife."

The kiss he gave her left her shaken. Despite all her pride, she realized she was drawn to this stranger she had married more than to any man she had ever known. Did he know? If he did, there was no sign of it.

Twilight, Jeff, and Ann were congratulating them, kissing them and wishing them well. Tears of happiness were in Twilight's eyes. Jenny, this little sister whom she loved so much, was married! And to what a man! Outside of her own Jeff, Twilight thought Dr. Reeves — Lance, she reminded herself — stood out above other men head and shoulders. She would bet on his fairness, honesty, moral fiber, in a world of indifference. Jenny would be cared for all her life.

Twilight turned a look of love on her own Jeff. Even after four years of marriage, each day was a new experience. Their love was so much deeper than it had been at first. She offered a quick petition that Jenny and Lance might find it so.

Jeff turned to them. "If we're going to start to Stehekin, we'd better get going. We'll make Chelan tonight — I have reservations for us — and catch the early morning *Lady of the Lake* tomorrow."

Sheer terror filled Jenny. She had forgotten they would have to stay overnight in Chelan. She had been looking forward to the peace and quiet of Aunt Lucy's Stehekin cabin. She need not have worried. Dr. Reeves was equal to any situation. In spite of her antagonism toward him, she felt admiration at the quick way he took care of anything that came up.

Almost apologetically, he looked at Jenny. "Darling, would you ever forgive me if I sent you on with your sister and I came tomorrow?" He turned to Twilight, Ann, and Jeff. "I know this is terrible, but there is an opportunity that won't come again. Just before I left the hospital, they told me a very old friend had come in with a terminal illness. He's not expected to make it through the night. Jenny," he implored, "I'd give anything to go with you, but this man took care of me for a long time. There's no point in your staying here in Seattle, since I'll be at the hospital all night. Go on with your sister. But if you say the word, I'll come with you."

Jenny's mental prayer of thankfulness didn't slow down her words. "Oh no, you *must* stay! After all, we have the rest of our lives. I would never forgive myself if I kept you from him."

The wistfulness in her voice was convincing. To make it extra good, she added, "Of course, you know how much I'll miss you. Come home soon, dear." Her melting tones faded at the blaze that leaped to Dr. Reeves's eyes, and for a moment she thought she had gone too far. But he only smiled.

"Then I'll bid my bride good-bye for just a day or so."

With the masterfulness so characteristic of him, he caught her close and, just before kissing her again, whispered softly, "Don't rock the boat, my dear, don't rock the boat!"

In a moment he was gone, leaving Jenny scarlet-faced in her bridal white, wondering just what he had meant by that cryptic comment. But not for long. They had a long journey ahead of them. It was time to change from the lovely lace gown, gather up her beautiful roses, and start out on a new life. With chin high, she waved good-bye to the Matthewsons, in the doorway of the vine-covered chapel, and Ann, who would follow them in a week or so, and courageously moved forward into the next chapter of her life.

Chapter 3

If Jenny could have known the state of Dr. Lancelot Reeves's feelings when he loudly replied, "I do!" she would have turned and run from the chapel, regardless of the confusion behind her. She little suspected that, for the first time in his life, Dr. Reeves was totally, unqualifiedly, in love — with her! When she had blazed at him a few days before in the hospital dining room, he had admired her. When she had accepted his spur-of-the-moment challenge and promised to marry him, he had loved her. When he had kissed her to provide a smoke screen for her family, he had worshipped her.

How the mighty are fallen, he thought to himself with a grim smile as he drove away from the chapel and his new bride, the bride he had promised would be his working partner only. And that's the way it is going to be, he promised himself. She told me there was no other man in her life. I would have known that anyway. She is as shy as a wild fawn, as pure and untouched as an avalanche lily.

I never thought there was such a thing as love at first sight, he mused. Yet every muscle, nerve, and heartbeat proclaimed his caring for this girl Jenny. When he had seen her walking down the aisle toward him in that white gown, wearing his ring, carrying his roses, for a moment he had wondered how life could be so good to him. What had ever happened in his life to merit such a choice gift as the brown-haired, brown-eyed beauty whose cold little hand slipped into his own? His heart had threatened to burst as they took their vows, vows he knew she would keep. He was honest enough to admit that as yet, as she had reminded him, she detested the situation. Yet the honor that had caused her to pledge herself to him for the sake of her people would surely in time bring her to love him! Until that day, his would be the comradeship part to play, teaching her to trust him, to be real friends. In short, to make up for all the time they would have spent together had he dated her in the usual way.

And what a setting! If Stehekin were only half as wild and beautiful as she had enthusiastically described it, then nature was on his side! He remembered her tale of how she and Twilight had been lost, and how she had given out, only to have Twilight face a wild bear on her behalf. He would gladly face a bear — in fact, it might be easier to face wild animals than to face Jenny herself, he thought wryly. She could really be to the point! Yet wasn't it that very quality that had brought him to where he now was?

The same thought recurred later that night when the hospital was quiet and all seemed lonely and still in the room of his old friend. The story he had told was true; he had not only been making a way out of an uncomfortable situation for both Jenny and himself. The shallow breathing of the old man was an indication of how near the end was. Yet earlier, the man had told Lance he was ready to go into the next world. He had lived a long life and now he wanted to join Mama, his beloved wife of over fifty years, who had passed on a few months before. How strange it was! So often when one of an old couple died, the other followed shortly. With the new awareness of what real love could be, Lance could understand it. His world would turn black if he lost Jenny now. What would it be like after so many years of companionship, accepting both the good and the bad, loving, living, bearing children, facing life always together?

The hospital that knew Dr. Lance Reeves would have been amazed at his ideals. In spite of all the divorce and so-called free love, he clung to the memory of his own mother and father and the beauty of the relationship they shared. He had sworn never to marry at all if he could not have the same. Now he was plunged head-long into marriage on such an unusual basis he couldn't help but grin to himself. What would that same father and mother think?

They would approve, he reassured himself. Anyone knowing Jenny would see she is the soul of honor. If I'm not man enough to win her, then I don't deserve her! He came from a long line of fighting ancestors, men and women who strove for happiness. Was he any less of a fighter? For a while when he came back from that training camp with his hand so badly hurt, he had just about given up. Day after day he had taught his dull classes, wishing he could be about the business of healing. Then had come the challenge of a woman about half his size.

The man in the bed stirred, sighed, and opened his eyes.

"Glad you're here, Doc. So tired. Must rest. See you in the morning." Another smile, a brightening of the eyes, and he was gone. How many times had Dr. Reeves seen the same thing, a quickening of the spirit, a look of joy, then death. How could anyone be a doctor, or a nurse, he amended hastily, and not believe there was more to life than was lived on earth? Pulling the sheet up over his old friend's face, he quietly went out, closing the door behind him. He signed the chart for the nurse, giving the time of death, and slowly left the hospital.

He hadn't realized how tired he was. His left hand ached with the tension and the stress he had been under the past few days. Yet that was a good sign. The aching showed that the muscles were starting to heal. He was too tired to even shower, or to think over the days ahead, but he had trained himself to sleep whenever the opportunity arose. It was broad daylight, the sun was streaming through the window, when he awoke and prepared to pack his personal belongings.

When had he taken time off for a drive such as he now took? It seemed eons in the past. From the time he left Seattle, all the way through beautiful Stevens Pass, he sang, whistled, and waved at other travelers.

Most of them look back at me as if I were nuts — maybe I am, he thought. But if this is what it's like to be nuts, I'm all for it. Then he couldn't help but laugh aloud at his assumption.

When he crossed the actual pass, he couldn't help but contrast the freedom, the lack of people, with the hustle-bustle of Seattle. Would he be bored out here in some godforsaken place? But Jenny, Twilight, and Jeff didn't feel it was godforsaken. Far from it. They thought it was probably God's country itself. His anticipation mounted. He stopped for gas and a bite to eat in Leavenworth, noting how it had been turned into a replica of a Bavarian village.

"I'll bring Jenny here," he resolved. "Surely if she'd ever spent any time here, she would have mentioned it." But now his anxiety to reach Chelan itself outweighed the charm of the small town.

Lake Chelan proved to be beautiful. He found accommodations without too much trouble, although the little town seemed crowded. Fortunately the barge was going up the lake the next day. His car would be safely delivered to Stehekin. He thanked the far-seeing fate that had caused him to purchase a station wagon several months earlier, rather than the sports car he had been considering. It was ideally suited to the area where he would be practicing.

The lake trip was beautiful. He was fascinated by the small hamlets along the way, especially Lucerne. He wished Jenny was with him, she loved it so. He would like to see it through her eyes.

But when he reached Stehekin and she came running to the dock to meet him, it was worth the wait. Of course it was to impress the crowd gathered to meet the boat, he told himself, but did her lips cling a bit as she greeted him with a kiss? There was no mistaking the pride she had in showing off her beloved Stehekin. Introductions were a jumble. It seemed everyone there must meet the boat!

Only a few names and faces stood out, but in time he would sort them out. Two that did stand out were Aunt Lucy and Jingles, a middle-aged couple who appeared to be so in love. Jenny had told him the story of their early love and their separation, and how they were reunited just when she came to Stehekin for the first time. Jingles's handclasp was hard, taking measure of "Jenny's young man." But approval filled his glance as Dr. Lance, as Jenny had introduced him, met his gaze squarely.

"You take good care of her," the older man directed.

There was satisfaction in Lance's being able to answer from the bottom of his heart, "I will." It was almost as if he were repeating his wedding vow. But Jenny, excited as she was, failed to catch the depth, as did Jingles.

"He's a good one," Jingles told Aunt Lucy as they started home, leaving Jenny eagerly directing Lance to the road that led to Aunt Lucy's old cabin among the trees, out of town.

Lance couldn't know how she had worked getting that cabin into shape for him. She was determined to keep her part of the bargain by taking as good care of him as possible, making sure he had no cause to dislike Stehekin. Jumping from the station wagon without waiting for his assistance, she dashed up the walk and flung wide the door, stepping inside to hold it open for him. Had she done so to prevent him carrying her across the threshold? Lance wondered, but he kept the thought to himself.

"It's perfect!" He couldn't have pleased her more. Indeed it was. Small, perfectly proportioned, the cottage, with its pine walls, ruffled curtains, and huge bearskin rug before the fireplace, was indeed the honeymoon cottage he had called it. Cocking his head at Jenny's nervous chatter, he realized the aroma that had assailed his nostrils on entering was a combination of fresh apple pie, homemade bread, and wood smoke. How refreshing! All that kept him from telling Jenny then and there that he loved her was his promise to himself. Instead, he laughed and sniffed again.

"Not only have I gained a beautiful wife, but she can even c-o-o-k!" It was the perfect icebreaker.

Jenny settled into a chair and pointed to the bearskin rug. Looking at him, she said, "And that is the rug that Jingles's grandson Tommy turned the bear that chased Twilight into!" Her odd choice of phrasing set them both into a fit of laughter, but Jenny couldn't help but add, "Well, anyway, you know what I mean."

Lance didn't trust himself so soon to settle down and visit with her, so he started for the door. "I'll bring in my lares and penates."

For a moment Jenny was still, some of her radiance gone. Then she rose and led him to one of the two bedrooms. "This is Aunt Lucy's. That is, yours."

Not for a moment did Lance betray himself. "Fine," he agreed heartily. "There's a dandy closet to stow away all my extra gear." He could hear Jenny's carefully held breath expelled in relief at his reply.

Deliberately whistling a catchy tune, he strode back and forth, back and forth, until the little room was filled to bursting with his things. He could hear Jenny in the kitchen, working with dishes, and soon she called him, a bit timidly, "Dinner's ready." He remembered how she had told him that up here it was "breakfast, dinner, supper" rather than "breakfast, lunch, dinner," as in the city.

"Boy, does that ever look good!" His wholehearted compliment brought a pleased look to the girl's eyes.

For a moment she hesitated while he held her chair, then asked shyly, "Do you mind if we say grace?"

He stared at her, his mind flashing back over the years to his own family, who always thanked God for their food. This marriage would be tricky enough; they needed all the help they could find. When he spoke, he asked, "Would you like us to take turns, and I can begin now?"

Happiness filled her eyes. She hadn't known how he would feel about it, but her

52

own faith was so strong it seemed even such an odd marriage as theirs should include gratefulness.

His words were simple, but they brought a mist of feeling to Jenny's eyes. "Father, we thank You for this food. May we be worthy of Thy love. May we be guided by Thee. Amen."

The little pool of feeling was broken by his adding, "Those biscuits look mighty good, Jenny. Let's try them!" But the look of reverence in his eyes haunted Jenny long after he had gone back to his unpacking and she had dried the last dish and put it away.

"Jenny, is it all right to put some of my medical books in those shelves by the fireplace? There isn't too much room in here."

"Of course." She came to the open door of his room, dishcloth still in hand. She hesitated to go in, but suddenly he wheeled toward her.

"Jenny." His tone was kind, but undemanding. "I don't want you to feel unnatural around me. Let's forget the strange marriage we have entered into for a while. I want you to feel free with me, the same kind of freedom you have with Twilight or Aunt Lucy. I can't have you starting every time I speak to you. We're partners, gal, partners! Don't you remember?" It took everything within him to speak the words, but it had to be done.

Instantly she caught his wish to put her at ease, his knowledge of her feelings now that she was alone with him, married to almost a complete stranger. Coming close she held out her hand, but as an effort to show her appreciation, she felt it a cold gesture. Instead she told him, "I will, Lance," and reached up to kiss his cheek in gratitude. She was amazed at his reaction.

"Don't do that!"

"Well, you needn't be so touchy. I was only —"

He interrupted. "It's all right, Jenny. Sorry." Then, turning the conversation completely, he said, "Come on, woman. Help me get these books moved."

Lights burned late in the little cabin that night. It had taken a long time to put away all the things Lance had managed to stow into his station wagon. Then, too, they had taken time out for an inspection trip to the tiny clinic the people had built with their hopes of attracting a doctor. It was shining and new, spotless. What it lacked in equipment it made up for in cleanliness, and for a small space, it was surprisingly adequate.

"I had been going to use it for a first-aid-type station," Jenny told Lance on their way home. "Now it can be a real clinic, as it deserves to be." In spite of the smart of his rebuff of her earlier friendly gesture, Jenny had determined not to let the new understanding between them be lost. She waited while Lance put the station wagon in the shed and checked the locks, although, as she told him, "Why we're doing this I'll never know. No one has to lock anything up here, especially away from town!" He couldn't help but marvel. He hadn't known there was anywhere left on earth so free from greed.

Just before putting the last lights out, he looked at her intently.

"Jenny, I have to tell you this. I've fallen in love."

Why should his words thrust themselves red hot into her soul? Jenny furiously demanded of herself. Trying to overcome the effects of her heart having nearly stopped for a moment, she coolly asked, "Oh?"

He seemed unaware of her perturbation. "Yes, totally and gloriously in love. When you described Stehekin, I thought it couldn't be so wonderful as your description. But you didn't do it justice, Jenny! I'm in love with it. I wouldn't mind spending most of the rest of my life here, just taking vacations now and then. Would you?"

The blessed relief of his answer caught her throat, and for a moment she couldn't reply. But it was long enough for him to add harshly, "I'm sorry. I had no right to ask that question." Turning to his own room, he called back over his shoulder, "Good night, Jenny. See you in the morning."

For a moment she stared at his closed door, floods of emotion threatening to overwhelm her. She could not account to herself why the thought that he had fallen in love had shaken her so, but it had. Quietly she made her way to her own room, undressing in the dark.

But it was many long, sleepless hours later before her eyes closed. What had she done? What if he eventually did fall in love with a worthy woman? He was tied to her, or did he believe that divorce was the answer to anything that stood in one's way? She couldn't quite reconcile that attitude with his face when he had said grace over their first meal together. Well, he didn't love anyone right now, or he surely wouldn't have married her. And there was no one in Stehekin who would attract his attention, at least for the present. Smiling to herself without quite knowing why such an immense amount of satisfaction came with the idea, Jenny slept. For the time being she was free of the shackles that bound her in a loveless marriage. She had decided to leave the future alone and take one day at a time.

And down the hall in Aunt Lucy's former room, Lance smiled to himself. She must not hate him completely or he wouldn't have received that kiss. His smile was replaced by a scowl. Wretch, to snap at her as he had! She couldn't know that his restraint had been near the breaking point. Leave the future alone, he told himself savagely. Take one day at a time. The thought steadied him, and soon he, too, was asleep.

The wise old moon smiled at the little cabin as if knowing secrets he would not share, but inside, the two who seemed at such cross purposes had given their worries over to the lullaby of the soft night wind.

Chapter 4

There was a Sunday hush over the world when Jenny awoke. Never had she felt so perfectly content. She lay still, savoring the moment. It had been a little over a week since she and Lance had started on the ocean of matrimony in their hastily constructed boat. In that time, she had seen him take charge of the clinic, using all the skill that had been legendary at the hospital. If it had not been for the still-weak hand, he could have handled anything that could ever possibly come up.

And yet it was because of that hand that Jenny herself was so important. Her two small, quick hands eased the load and turned the trick under his supervision. Never had she worked with anyone with such perfect teamwork as with Lance. It was beautiful.

Their worth had been proven even in the short time they had been home. Tourists afflicted with various kinds of problems; an old neighbor who had been putting off getting down to Chelan for an eye examination and who turned out to have beginning glaucoma, still early enough to be treated and cured; a broken leg set for one of the National Park Service employees — the list went on and on.

"I did the right thing," the girl whispered to herself, her lips curving into a smile. She gazed at the rings on her left third finger, remembering also how the few days had seemed to begin their magic work with Lance. Despite the busy schedule, there had been time to drive as far up the valley as the road went. He had been thrilled with its beauty. The dark trees, the pure blueness of the unpolluted air, the sunshine and birds and flowers, all lent themselves to the enchantment of Stehekin Valley. When a deer and two fawns stepped out, seemingly unafraid, and looked at them, the look on Lance's face was payment enough for the doubts and fears that Jenny had sometimes had in the dark hours of the night when things had looked the gloomiest. Now she could face those doubts, refusing to dwell on what might be or what had been and concentrate on living for the moment.

Today was to be a special day. After services in the old Golden West Lodge, there was to be a community reception for

Lance and Jenny. Twilight had insisted that Jenny should wear her lace wedding dress, but Jenny demurred. However, later she thought it over and a little hesitantly approached Lance with the casual comment, "Twilight thought I should wear my wedding dress. Don't you think that's silly?"

He looked at her in surprise. "Silly? That's the most beautiful dress in the world! Wear it." Before she could catch her breath at his unexpected praise, he had quickly turned and gone back into the clinic.

As she lay in bed watching the first searching fingers of early morning steal through the trees and into her window, Jenny treasured the remark. She would wear the dress if it pleased him so much. Since the first night he arrived at Stehekin he had been scrupulously careful about upholding his part of their bargain. Gradually she had learned to relax and accept him as he had asked, as a partner, a dear friend. If at times she suspected he might be laughing at her, never by word or deed did he confirm it.

"Jenny, are you awake?" The knock at her door sent her deeper under the covers.

"Y-yes, Lance."

"It's such a beautiful morning! Why don't we get ready for church and drive over and surprise Aunt Lucy and Jingles for breakfast? We can always come back and change before the reception."

"Sounds great!" Jenny was out of bed in a flash. Before long, they were in the station wagon and driving into the sunrise that threatened to set the world afire with its brilliance. First the rosy touch of pink chiffon, then old rose enamel, followed by streaks of crimson, ruby, and clear orange. Never had Lance seen such a sunrise! He stopped the car, and they got out to savor the beauty for a moment.

"Red sky in the morning, sailor take warning," Jenny chanted. Her cheeks were as red as the sky, and her brown eyes had caught the sunlight's brilliance. In her soft green outfit, she seemed part of the woods, a wild thing, such as the butterfly hovering on a nearby wild rose.

"Say, wife, you're beautiful today!" Lance kept his tone light as he gave the compliment in such a way she could not take offense.

"Thank you kindly, sir, she said," Jenny returned, making a deep curtsy, then running ahead. If they were to make breakfast at the Jacobsens', they would have to get going again.

"Welcome, welcome!" Jingles stood on the steps of the ranch house. His words seemed to be repeated by the soft whinny of horses in the nearby corral. Lance appreciated those fine animals, which Jingles used to take parties into the mountains. When things were different with Jenny, he wanted to do that very thing, take a pack trip away from even the slightly used areas. Now he shook his head. He had best be thankful for Jenny's lessening wariness, not be making plans for what might transpire!

It was a Sunday to remember, one to press close and cherish as one would press and cherish some long-ago flower in an album. From the hearty breakfast they went to Stehekin boat landing and the old Golden West Lodge.

The lodge fascinated Lance, as did the minister who came in from the "outside." This morning his text was, "Ask and ye shall receive; seek and ye shall find; knock and it shall be opened unto you."

Here was no watered-down, one-day-a-week religion. Here was a living, vibrant belief that God wanted to work *with* man, not just *for* him.

"Is there something in your life too big to handle? Something you feel you can't solve, no matter how hard you try? Ask. Seek. Find. Help is there, but God's hands are tied unless you take that first faltering step toward Him. When you do, He is bound to keep His promises. There is no hurt too large for Him to heal. . . ."

Unconsciously, Lance rubbed his left hand with his right. Jenny noticed the gesture and impulsively laid her own hand over his. She was rewarded by a smile from the depth of the blue eyes that could be icy as the lake on a stormy day or as clear as the heavens. It was a moment of sharing in which she reiterated her faith that his hand would be taken care of in time.

The reception would always stand out in both of their memories. Even though Lance had met many of the people during the week, now there was opportunity to stop and visit. Against the background of wildflowers that Twilight and Ann, who had arrived breathlessly the day before, had arranged, Jenny's white dress stood out. Could she have become more beautiful even since their wedding? Lance demanded of himself. Yes, she was. That day she had been troubled, uncertain. Today she was confident, radiant, at home. For a moment he felt an outsider. And yet, wasn't he fulfilling all her dreams of medical help for Stehekin? Putting aside gloomy thoughts, he listened to her chatter as she told him a little about each family who came to wish them well.

"It's hard to believe it's been four years," she exclaimed. "Yet now I see how that first class of Twilight's has grown!" She gestured to the Jacobsen children. Tommy, still freckled and towheaded, was fourteen. Honey, as blonde and petite as her name, ten. Twilight's three eighth graders — Frank Wilson, Jr.; Columbine Jones, as fair as the wildflower for which she was named; and Mike Cummings, son of Miles, who was a National Park Service employee — had just graduated from high school in Chelan. They were back for the summer, trying to decide what came next in their lives. Lance was amused at the two boys trying to outdo themselves for Columbine. He couldn't blame them. She was just as gracious and sweet in personality as in face and form.

Then there was Tara Wilson, as questioning as she had been in first grade; Pixie and Rusty Jones, who were now seventh and eighth graders respectively. Penny and Pam, the Richards twins were no longer in Stehekin. They had moved the year after Twilight's advent, to the tune of loud wails, Twilight told Jenny. What a fine group of young people, Lance thought. He contrasted them with some of the teen-agers, and some even younger, who had been brought into the hospital in Seattle. Drug victims, accident victims from combining alcohol and fast driving in a furious effort to belong, to get kicks from life. It all seemed far away.

With an effort, he recalled himself to the present. Jingles, who, as usual, was the spokesman for the group, had called for silence. Lifting high his glass of lemonade, he proposed a toast to the new bride and groom.

"May you ever find as much happiness in life as you are giving others." The sincere words brought mist to Jenny's eyes and a lump as big as a baseball to Lance's throat. Unknown to each other, each offered a quick silent prayer that Jingles's words would prove true. But he wasn't through.

"We thought it all over and didn't know what you might like. Instead of going out and buying you something for your house, or each of us picking out something that would probably be of no earthly use, we decided to go together for a wedding present." He withdrew a long envelope from his pocket.

"Maybe you can use this for something in the clinic. It's yours to use as you see fit." There was an old-fashioned courtliness in his little speech, and with trembling fingers Jenny took the cashier's check from the envelope. Her gasp was audible.

"Five hundred dollars!" She stared at them with the same amazement that Lance felt. The small group before them had given five hundred dollars to them! It was too much for Jenny. Bursting into tears, she could only hold out the check to Lance. "I don't know what to say — it's so much!"

Lance, too, was at a loss for words, but Jingles saved the day.

"Well," he drawled. "If you think it's too much for a wedding present, you can consider part of it a bribe to keep you here!" The howl of laughter that followed successfully dried Jenny's eyes.

Recovering her usual poise, she could answer, "You don't know what this will mean. We can use it for some equipment that could really be of value here." Again her voice broke, but this time Lance could help her out.

"Some of my friends have wanted to know what we wanted." He ignored Jenny's quick intake of breath. She hadn't once thought of his friends and how they would naturally want to give him gifts on his wedding.

"I'll tell them of your gift and ask them if they'd like to add to it. Knowing the hospital bunch, we will come up with enough money to get some really fine equipment."

Jenny's heart swelled with pride. What a man she had married! She could almost fall in love with him just for his generosity. Disciplining a laugh, she led him to the great cake, and they continued going through all the motions of a reception. In one way it seemed so phony, so deceptive. Yet on the other hand, the happiness in the faces around Jenny soothed the conscience that accused her of living a lie. No one was being hurt, she assured herself, watching Lance laughing with Ann and Miles Cummings. Ann looked lovely in a sea-green dress and, as usual, fitted into the picture as if an artist had painted her there. It was one of her talents, being part of any group.

Jenny had not had an opportunity to

really talk with Ann. They had all been so busy since she arrived. But Jenny could see the girl was happy and wide-eyed over the beauty of Stehekin. In a way, Jenny dreaded the explanations that would have to follow. But she had reckoned without Ann's keen sense of awareness. Neither then nor in days to follow did Ann ask Jenny anything. She simply accepted the way things were. The hospital in Seattle might have been located in a previous incarnation in Afghanistan as far as Ann was concerned. What mattered was that Jenny and Lance were married, and to all appearances, very happy. They were both tanned, rested. It was enough for Ann.

The reception was over. The last crumb of cake had been eaten, the last bit of lemonade and coffee consumed. Jenny felt curiously let down.

Lance sensed something of this and suggested, "How about going home for a change of clothes and hiking somewhere?" Her face brightened immediately. She loved the trails. But by this time she knew enough not to go off the trail after ferns and flowers, as she had once when she had first come there. It was easy to lose one's way in an unfamiliar forest.

When they reached home, she was out of

the wagon and up the walk before he could help her. Again he wondered if it were deliberate, to foil his carrying her across the threshold, this time in bridal white. But the eager face that turned toward him a little later as they stepped out in walking shoes and casual clothes convinced him otherwise. What a girl! His admiration grew daily. She was everything he had ever longed for, dreamed of. Outstanding as a nursing helper. A wonderful cook and housekeeper in spite of the time she gave to her work with him.

He had fallen into the habit of helping with the night dishes. Over the sudsy water they discussed the day's cases.

At first she had protested. "That's woman's work!"

"My dear girl!" His tone was shocked; mock horror filled his blue eyes. "You mean to tell me, in this day and age, you still separate work into man's and woman's? Shades of the nineteenth century, but you're behind the times!" Abandoning his pose, he told her seriously, "You're just as busy during the day as I am. I'll help at home."

Seeing she still wasn't convinced, he added, "Besides, that hot water is good for my hand. It helps relax those tight muscles." It was true. Every day Lance's hand was getting better. Jenny wasn't too sure if the dishwater had anything to do with it, but she rejoiced that his hand was improving.

As they set out for their walk, the stillness of the forest closed in around them. After they had walked a little way, Lance dropped onto a stump. Looking at Jenny intently, he asked, "Jenny, today at the reception you seemed so carefree, so happy. Would it be all right if I asked you a question?"

Why should his grave tones strike a somber warning bell in her mind? She could see he was deadly serious.

"Go ahead." She kept her own voice as emotionless as possible.

"I wondered — was it all put on for the benefit of Stehekin?" He raised his hand to stop her answer. "Wait. Let me finish." But he dropped into silence for such a long time that Jenny couldn't help but wonder what on earth was coming. When it did, she didn't know how to respond.

"Do you still despise me?" he asked.

It took her so by surprise, and set her heart thumping so, she couldn't speak. In the distance the ring of a cowbell proclaimed evening was near, cows were going home for milking. One lone nighthawk circled above them. A little brown rabbit paused to survey the silent couple, then made his own way home to a waiting family. Even the chipmunks and squirrels ceased their chattering. The whole world seemed to wait for Jenny's answer, but none so intently as Lance, whose knuckles clenched white.

"Despise you?" Jenny's eyes were as honest and transparent as the deep pool bordered by green ferns nearby. "I respect you with all my heart."

Lance swallowed hard, and when he spoke his voice was husky. "Thank you, Jenny." It was all he could manage.

Jenny's answer had been short and direct, yet it was enough to show him his program of self-discipline was reaping a harvest like none he had ever coveted before. She could not have chosen words that would have glowed in his heart more than those few.

Chapter 5

Summer is nearly over, Jenny thought as she flexed the muscles of her shoulders, stiff from the long day's work at the clinic. Unconsciously she sighed. She was tired, perhaps more tired than she had ever been before.

She spoke without looking at Lance, who was washing up before going home. "I'll be glad when the summer season is over and most of the tourists are gone."

For a moment he didn't answer, and when he did, it was with a laugh. "Don't forget, woman, those same tourists provided bread and butter for us this summer."

Jenny swung away from the window where she had been watching the leaves, noticing that already the crisp nights had begun to touch them with color. "I know," she told him penitently. "But lately it seems it's been one accident after another! We no sooner got that lady with the heart attack comfortable than Jingles brought in the little girl who had fallen from her horse. Then" — counting on her fingers — "of all the times for summer flu to hit! I think half the valley is down with it." She brushed her heavy hair back from her forehead.

Instantly Dr. Lance was at her side. "You aren't feeling too well yourself, are you, Jenny?" In spite of her protests, he slipped a thermometer under her tongue and felt for her pulse.

"Just as I thought. A hundred and one. We've got to get you to bed right away." A frown crossed his face. "I don't want you home alone when I'm not there, and I can't close the clinic, as busy as it is."

Leaning against the examining table for balance, unwilling to let him see how ill she really felt, Jenny said, "Twilight has room for me. She'd be glad to look after me for a few days." The world was spinning. Strange, this flu virus. It worked so rapidly! She had felt fine that morning, but at lunch her head had ached. She had attributed it to the long day, but now an all-gone feeling pervaded her entire being.

She managed to say, "I think Ann would come up and help you out for a few days," before Lance caught her up, protesting, carried her through the door that automatically locked behind them, and bundled her off to Twilight's.

Twilight took one look at her sister and ordered Lance to bring Jenny in, but Aunt Lucy came to the doorway and stopped them with a command.

"No, Lance! Not here. Bring her to Jingles and me." She raised a hand against Twilight's outcry. "You have to think of your baby, Twilight. No sense exposing yourself needlessly. We'll take care of her."

Lance agreed. "It's only a few weeks until your baby is due. Jenny will be fine with Aunt Lucy."

His genuine smile warmed the older lady's heart, but she only returned, in her somewhat prickly manner that didn't fool anyone, even herself, "Huh, she ought to be! I've been taking care of folks a good many years. Never lost one to flu yet, even if I'm not an M.D." Jenny was too sick to care. She only remembered the softness of the quiet upstairs room in the ranch house, and the tenderness with which Lance and Aunt Lucy tucked her in.

"Such a fuss to make over a little flu bug," she croaked, her throat starting to grow sore and scratchy. "I'm just tired. I'll be all right."

In two minutes she was sound asleep. Did she dream Lance's gentle touch on her flushed cheek, or did he really whisper, "Take care, my darling"? Of course not. He didn't love her. Or did he? It was all mixed up in her mind.

The next three days were jumbled. The virus had to run its course, and Jenny's fever proved to be stubborn. It wasn't until the morning of the fourth day that she awakened clearheaded, smiling at Aunt Lucy, who had entered with a tray. "I'm hungry enough to eat a bear!"

Her aunt laughed. "Not all at once. Try this toast and broth first, and we'll see about the bear next." Jenny wrinkled her nose. She had always hated so-called invalid food. She felt ravenous enough to demand eggs, bacon, orange juice, and hotcakes.

Aunt Lucy forestalled her, seeing the gleam in the patient's eyes. "This is what the doctor ordered."

Jenny couldn't help but laugh, and she ate her toast and broth. It was surprisingly good. "Can I get up?"

Aunt Lucy nodded. "If you feel like it, Dr. Lance said for a little while." There was amusement in her eyes. "I'm sure I don't know what he would have done if Ann hadn't been here to help him. He spent so much time running back and forth out here checking on you, I don't see how he took care of any patients!" Jenny was wide-eyed. She hadn't known he had been there so much. It was hard to remember, through her fever.

"Jenny, I've been wanting to talk with you. You know how Jake and I care about you."

Jenny smiled at the "Jake" — Aunt Lucy was the only one who could get away with calling Jingles by his given name.

For once Aunt Lucy had put aside her brusque manner. Settling herself in the rocker by the bed while Jenny finished eating, she opened feelings to Jenny in a way the girl hadn't associated with her aunt, beloved as she was. Somehow one didn't expect Aunt Lucy to talk as she now did. Her busy hands, never still, mended a torn dress for Honey while she spoke.

"Jenny, I have to tell you what a wonderful man you married." Peering over the glasses she wore for close work, she saw the telltale red stain coloring the girl's cheeks, unusually pale from her illness.

"Oh, you needn't blush and think you know it yourself!" For a long moment the busy fingers were still. "When I married Jake and when Twilight and Jeff were married, I didn't think there was another man left in the world good enough for you. You know that you and Twilight are all the children I ever had, until I took over Tommy and Honey the same time as I did Jake." Much to Jenny's amazement, a tear slipped down Aunt Lucy's laugh-wrinkled cheek.

"Many's the time I prayed that God would be with you. All the time you were in training and doing that heavy work, I thought of you and rejoiced that the surgery hadn't damaged your heart but strengthened it, so you could serve. Then when you and Lance came here, so young and happy, it was an answer to all those prayers." Jenny's lashes swept down over her eyes. Not for a million dollars could she have answered. We must be performing our deception successfully, she thought to herself, a bitter note in the idea.

But Aunt Lucy hadn't stopped. "Lance loves you so very much, Jenny, so very much. May you always cherish that love."

The door closed behind her. Evidently Jenny's downcast eyes had lured her into thinking her niece was tired. It was well she left. As soon as the door closed, Jenny's eyes popped wide open. Loved her? Lance loved her? Aunt Lucy must be wrong. In the summer days of working together, they

77

had developed a good relationship, become friends, partners. But love?

Jenny slid deeper into the soft, protective comfort of the patchwork quilt Aunt Lucy had made. Her face flamed. What if it were true? She didn't want to face that thought. If she did, then she had to consider her own truant feelings, and she wasn't ready for that, not yet. But as she slipped back into sleep, there was a kind of wonder in her mind. Could it be true? Aunt Lucy was a good judge of human relationships.

The same thought caused her to feel a little ill at ease when Lance came that night. Jenny was propped up on the downstairs sofa, wearing a yellow housecoat that brought out highlights of her shining brown hair. Aunt Lucy had helped her brush it and tie it back with a scrap of yellow ribbon she produced from her work basket. The ribbon was probably the former property of Honey, who sat on the end of the sofa, Jenny's protective slave.

Lance was hearty in his approval. "You're doing fine! One more day with Aunt Lucy, and you should be as good as new. But I think you'd best plan to take a week or so off from the clinic."

He turned to smile broadly at Ann, who had followed him in. Her uniform and cap were as crisp and white as if she hadn't worked all day. In spite of her thankfulness that this good friend had come up to help, Jenny felt a little resentful. How could she look like that after a busy day? Jenny herself usually felt like a dishrag until she could get home and shower!

Stop being ridiculous, she told herself furiously, but in spite of her admonition a little of the hurt crept into her voice as she asked, "Don't you want me?"

For a moment Lance stared at her, noting the droop to her lips, the unasked question in the big, brown eyes. He stifled an impulse to cross the room, and tell her just exactly how much he did want her, and not just at the clinic, either. Restraining himself, he took refuge in laughter.

"I want you home first, then at the clinic, good and well. In the meantime, Ann is doing a grand job, and she says she will stay as long as needed. In fact, Jenny, I've been trying to sell her on staying up here for a while. We can use her at least part-time, and when Twilight's baby comes . . ." He left the sentence unfinished. Jenny quickly put aside the little pang of jealousy at his wholehearted praise of her friend, so beautiful in the white outfit.

"That would be grand! Think what it would mean to Twilight! She will have her baby right here; we can trade off taking care of her and manning the clinic. Will you do it, Ann, please?"

"Besides," Lance put in, "what are all your followers going to think if you end your visit?"

"Followers?" Jenny had lost the train of conversation.

"Oh, Lance," Ann protested. She turned to Jenny. "Just because since you've been gone a lot of people have come in to 'get a look at the new nurse,' he thinks I have followers."

Lance didn't give up so easily. "Methinks the lady protests too hotly. What about that new Park Service ranger? The one Jeff brought in to get stitches in his hand?" Ann was effectively silenced. She *had* been impressed by the rangy man and the way he kept still as his hand was dressed. She had also caught the look of admiration in his eyes for her. But not for the world would she admit her own instant attraction.

"What *was* his name?" she asked innocently. "After all, we've been so busy . . ." Her nonchalance didn't fool Jenny.

Lance continued his teasing, "I think his

name is Romeo." With a wicked grin, he headed for the kitchen. "Hey, Aunt Lucy, is dinner about ready? I'm starved!"

"Hmm, certainly makes himself at home, doesn't he?" Ann demanded of Jenny. But making sure no one else could hear, she whispered, "His name is Don Parker, and he's as nice as any man I've ever seen!" Then she quickly slipped away before Jenny could respond.

So! The selective Ann had finally seen someone who really caught her interest! Jenny wasn't willing to admit why this fact had caused such relief in her heart. It could not be, of course, that it eased over the frank approval by Lance of Ann's work. She wasn't that much of a cat! After all, she herself didn't love Lance, did she? Why should she care if he admired another woman, even her best friend Ann? Sternly thrusting the thought away, she was glad to welcome Honey and her supper tray. They had insisted she stay on the sofa instead of trying to sit at the table just yet. This time, she wasn't on starvation rations. Dr. Lance had said she could eat whatever she wanted. And with that carte blanche, did she ever eat!

Could anyone fry chicken as Aunt Lucy did, never greasy, but crusty outside, tender inside? Or did any home-canned vegetables in the world taste as good as her aunt's? She must get Aunt Lucy to help her put up some for her own winter storehouse. Fresh vegetables were limited in winter, and home-canned ones would be very welcome.

That evening after Lance had gone back to the clinic to finish a report, Twilight and Jeff drove over to check on Jenny and to take Ann home. Even in her younger days, never had Twilight looked so beautiful as she did that evening. The great purple eyes were filled with happiness over the soon-approaching event. It shouldn't be over two or three weeks now. Her soft violet smock and deeper purple slacks did not accentuate her approaching motherhood, simply showed the great beauty that comes to a woman who loves, is loved, and looks forward to bearing her husband's child.

"You're really pretty tonight," Jingles told Twilight, who blushed. She stole an involuntary look at Jeff, whose quiet nod gave full approval of Jingles's compliment.

To hide her confusion, she stated, "I used to see so many women on campus who were expecting a baby and who walked around looking like the original instant mess that I decided if I ever was pregnant I'd make sure I didn't just let myself go!" A shout of laughter at the idea of Twilight letting herself go rocked the room, but she insisted, half seriously now.

"Really," she appealed to Ann and Jenny. "Don't you remember all those gals with their stringy hair, sloppy clothes, and bare feet who used to cross the campus lawns?" The girls had to admit they did. But to compare any of them with Twilight was almost heresy.

It was a happy evening, in spite of Lance's absence and Ann's sometime lapses into silence. Was she thinking of the big, kindly stranger? Jenny thought. But remembering how Ann had never once referred to the fact that she knew how short a time Lance and Jenny had known each other before their unexpected wedding, Jenny wisely kept her questions to herself. Ann was not one to be impaled on the pin of curiosity. When the time came and she was ready, she would tell Jenny.

A warm rush of love filled Jenny for this girl with whom she had lived four years of her life as roommate. Lifting her head, Ann caught the look and returned it warmly. Theirs was a special friendship. Never in the time they had known each other had they quarreled. Disagreed, yes, or it would have been four years of boredom. But no arguments had marred the time they spent together.

I'm really lucky, Jenny decided. Ann, Twilight, Jeff, Aunt Lucy and Jingles and the kids, Lance . . . But here she broke off.

"Good night, Jenny." It was blonde Honey patting her hand before trotting off to bed. Jenny had never seen a ten-year-old girl so willing to do what an adult told her.

"What's your secret?" Jenny demanded, and her aunt smiled.

"I overheard Jake talking to Honey and Tommy after we were first married. One of them had done something naughty. Instead of punishing, he sat down on the porch with one on each side.

" 'You know Aunt Lucy has come to live with us?' Both heads nodded. 'Then if we want her to stay, we'd better all three really be good and not worry her.' It was all he had to say. There's hardly ever been an incident since that couldn't be handled with a few quiet words from one of us."

Again Jenny marveled at the simple wisdom. Yet she knew it was more than that. Jingles and Aunt Lucy loved the children enough to discipline when really necessary. It was part of them and part of the children. Somewhere in the past Jenny had heard a favorite author express it, "with a rod of love." It certainly fit.

Slowly she went back upstairs, surprised at how tired she still became. But tomorrow . . . tomorrow she could go home!

It sometimes seemed Jenny's life came in segments. The next ten days were a segment she would cherish. She didn't go back to the clinic for a time. Lance had been right; she was still weak. If Ann hadn't been so capable, Jenny would have insisted. But as it was, she was free to enjoy that time. She used it in looking up new and tasty recipes. Lance never knew when he left in the morning just what she would have for his dinner that night.

Jenny sometimes felt as if she were back in her childhood days playing house, really enjoying the cooking, the little touches she made to the house, the unexpected drop-in visits from Aunt Lucy, the children, Twilight, and some of the neighbors. They all called the cabin the Doll House. Indeed, although Aunt Lucy had left it charming and Twilight and Jeff had added to it, it was left for Jenny to put on the finishing touches. There was hardly a day that some of the wildflowers still bravely raising their heads in defiance of the now ever-chilling evenings didn't grace the table. Lance would stand in amazement, the cares of his busy day put aside when he entered that home. He had hired a neighbor to bring a great load of wood, and when he wanted to get away from his mental strain, Lance would grab an axe and split logs. He waved away Jingles's offer of his small chain saw.

"This is helping my hand." Indeed, the muscles were becoming hard and firm, and it was difficult now to see if there was really much difference between the actions of the two hands. Besides, Lance was happy. In spite of his somewhat precarious footing with Jenny, every day seemed to bring them a little closer. He firmly believed that the winter, with its long cozy evenings before that fireplace, would finish the work his own self-control had begun. She was never self-conscious around him now as she had been at first. He caught a genuine fondness in her eyes when she didn't know he was watching.

I'm glad she wasn't one with a succession of romances in her life, he often thought. She is a pearl among women. Then he would laugh at himself for his poetic fancies and get back to work. But the little Doll House seemed to open its arms and shout, "Welcome!" each time he came home. One day he came home unexpectedly. Jenny evidently had gone out for a bit. Her apron lay on the kitchen table. There was no note. Of course, she wouldn't have expected him yet. He was amazed at his disappointment, out of all proportion to the little happening. The cottage was just as charming as ever, but it seemed cold, empty. It was Jenny, herself, who meant home.

One night in late September when the beautiful fall world had turned traitor and was dumping one of the worst storms of the season on them, Lance and Jenny were sitting before their crackling fire, the largest of the year to date. The orange and yellow flames, which changed to red and danced on the walls, seemed to shut out the storm. Lance was idly massaging his left hand, and Jenny was busily turning the hem of a pair of slacks that had been too long.

"Jenny?" She looked up, her smile catching at his heart. "Jenny, I think if I had to operate, I could."

She tossed down her work and clasped her hands together. Her face was radiant.

"Really, Lance?" There was no mistaking the joy in her eyes.

The man continued to watch her, then held up his hand. "It's been over a year since I've done an operation, but Stehekin seems to have done the trick. The hard work, the outdoors, maybe most of all the complete relaxation and contentment I've come to know here. It's all done its work well. I wouldn't attempt it yet, until I was more sure — unless it was an absolute emergency — but yes, Jenny, if I had to use it for surgery, I could."

She suddenly buried her face in her hands.

Startled from his own thoughts, he blurted out, "Jenny, you're crying!"

"So what? I guess I can cry if I want to!" There was belligerence in her voice. It was too much for Lance. All those weeks of iron self-control had brought him close to a breaking point.

Striding to her chair, he pulled her to her feet.

"Why should you care so much that I have the use of my hand again?"

The sternness of his face sent shivers up and down her spine. In another second she would have blurted out for the whole world to hear, "I love you!" But before the words were torn from her throat, a mighty pounding on the door drew them apart.

"Lance! Jenny!" It was Jeff's voice. Before they could go to the door, he was inside, dripping water all over the floor.

"It's Twilight, she's . . ." His voice failed, but instantly Lance responded.

"Don't worry. It's all right. Babies have a way of coming into this world at the most inconvenient times, such as in the middle of the night or during a bad storm." His matter-of-fact tone steadied Jeff.

"I dropped off Twilight and Ann at the clinic. Thought maybe she'd be better off there, and Ann said she'd start preparing her for delivery."

Lance nodded, head deep in the closet, snatching out his heavy jacket. Jenny put on heavy coat and boots and was ready by the time Lance had his medical bag. It wasn't far to the clinic, but the going was so slow it seemed they crawled! Wind and rain battered against the wagon. Never had Jenny been so glad as when she saw the lights of the clinic.

"Thank God we have our own generating system!" Lance's words were for Jenny alone, and her heart echoed the prayer. As usual before attending any patient, Jenny sent up a quick petition that she and Lance might be instruments in the hands of the Great Physician. Tonight it was her own sister, Twilight, who lay in the clinic needing help. God grant us steadiness, she asked, and felt comforted.

It didn't take long for them to examine Twilight. Thanks to Ann's efficient ministrations, she was all ready for them when they arrived. Neither did it take long for them to know that something was wrong. Twilight's lips had taken on a blue tinge, and her skin an unhealthy pallor. Her eyes were bright.

Lance left the little alcove where he had laid aside his equipment and went to the waiting room, motioning for Jenny to follow. The look on his face showed Jeff that something was wrong.

"What is it?" Jeff barely whispered.

"The baby is in the wrong position. She can't have a natural birth. She needs a Caesarean section."

"Here?" The word was uttered before Jenny could stop it.

Jeff's face turned even whiter. "Can you do it?"

Lance looked at him evenly. "I don't know. Just before you came I told Jenny I thought I could perform surgery if I absolutely had to, in an emergency. It's an emergency, all right. If Twilight were back in the city, there would be no problem. A Caesarean usually can be handled well. But here, with limited facilities, my uncertain hand? I honestly don't know, Jeff."

Jeff didn't hesitate a moment. "And the alternative?" he said.

It was quick in coming and the whole truth. "Death, for both Twilight and the baby."

"My God!" Jeff's broken face was so full of pain that Jenny turned away, but only momentarily.

Then she clutched her brother-in-law's arm. "We can save her, Jeff. I know we can. Ann and I will help. I can assist; Ann will anesthetize. But you're going to have to help, too, hard as it is. We're shorthanded. You can circulate. Now get scrubbed up!" She motioned to the basin visible through the partly open door, where Ann was already scrubbing.

Twilight's wide eyes were watching, but she made no sound. She sensed something was wrong, but had such confidence in those around her, she didn't question.

Jenny's words seemed to galvanize them into action. Lance drew a long breath. It had come, and in such a way as he had never expected! God help him that he might not fail!

He turned to Jeff. "You know I can't make any guarantee . . ." He never finished the sentence. Jeff's hard hand gripped his shoulder as he nodded, then followed Jenny into the other room.

She whispered as they entered, "Whatever you do, *don't look at Twilight!* Once the surgery is started, we'll tell you what to do, but don't look at her. If you do, you're going to forget everything except that it is your wife there, and that could make the difference for life and death for her."

Jeff was in control now. Jenny's words even helped him be able to smile at Twilight. "We're going to put you to sleep now, honey. When you wake up, you'll be a brand new mother!"

It was the last thing she heard, as the anesthetic took effect. She would never know the full extent of the fight that was made that night on behalf of her and the baby. The wind howled outside; the rain poured down. All the forces of heaven and earth seemed determined to outwit the four who fought so valiantly in that out-of-the-way corner of the world. But those forces at last abated, then died out completely, in the face of the determination in that little room. They could not withstand the triumph as a new life was lifted into this world and a mother was saved by surgeon's fingers that had all the grace and skill of former years.

Only once did those fingers tremble, and that was when the last clamp and stitch had been finished. Great beads of perspiration stood out on Lance's forehead, and now that her anesthetizing duties were over, Ann reached over and wiped them off. Jeff had been beautiful. Not until it was all over and he saw that not only was Twilight going to pull through but that he now had a brand new son did he give way to tears. Hastily brushing them aside, he almost ran to the waiting room, burying his face in Twilight's still-wet coat that no one had had time to hang up. Great, tearing sobs shook his big frame.

"Reaction," Lance told Jenny. Her eyes looked enormous above the white mask as she reached up to remove it. Even though Twilight would still need a lot of watching and care, it was over, Jenny thought dully. She could remember the sharp commands for instruments that Lance had snapped at her, the constant checking of blood pressure and pulse by Ann, the magnificent way Jeff had held up. Ann had slipped into the tiny kitchenette and in a minute was back with steaming cups of instant coffee. Although Jenny didn't usually like it, this was one time she gratefully accepted the hot cup. Ann forced Jeff to drink two cups, talking to him in a low tone. At last he was able to still his shaking hands.

"I don't know how to thank you," he started to say.

Lance's face, still grim from the strain he had been under, cut him short. "Then don't." His crooked smile took the sting from his words, and he stretched to full height.

Jenny had gone back to her sister's side. She and Lance would spend the night at the clinic in case Twilight . . . She refused to finish the thought. Surely nothing could happen now!

"Take Ann home so she can get some rest," Lance ordered Jeff. He shook his head at Jeff's involuntary protest. "You can't do anything for her tonight, and we're going to need Ann tomorrow. All three of us, plus you, can't take care of Twilight if we're worn out." When it was put on that basis, Jeff couldn't refuse. His nerves were still on edge, but at last he was starting to settle down.

"Why, it's cleared up!" Ann's exclamation drew them all to the door for a moment. It was true. An apologetic half moon had appeared, trailed by a single star, and these beamed congratulations at the tired group.

"Fair tomorrow from the looks of it." A tiny wail cut through their farewell; Thomas Jefferson Stone was announcing his right to their attention. There was still a long night to be fought through, a battle against possible infection. And yet there was only hope as the four soldiers of the clinic parted for the night. A few phrases from Jenny's graduation stood out in her mind: ". . . against poverty . . . heal, teach, and learn . . . because of you a soul returns to earth for a little while longer. . . ." Only tonight had she really known what those words meant.

Chapter 6

An errant ray of sunlight touched Jenny's tangled hair, flirted outrageously with the shining instruments in the case, and at last turned back to the girl and shone brightly at her eyes. Wearily she opened them, but in an instant she became fully awake. Twilight was doing fine, so Lance had insisted she curl up on the couch in the waiting room. It's a good thing I'm small, she thought, stretching. Even so, the couch had left her feeling she had slept on a bed of rocks.

Tiptoeing to the adjoining room, she saw for herself that both Twilight and the baby were sleeping normally. The terrific battle that had been fought the night before had paid off.

"Good morning!" There was gladness in Lance's voice as he took in the rumpled clothing, uncombed hair, and shining eyes of this remarkable girl who had married him so unorthodoxly.

Something of his feelings must have crept into that look, because she flushed and pushed back her shining fall of hair. "I must look a mess."

The man's eyes were dancing with merriment, but his tone was grave. "Well, let me see. There is a smudge on your left cheek, a scratch on your right arm, and . . ." Jenny interrupted him by marching firmly into the adjoining lavatory and making repairs.

When she returned, he told her, "You didn't stay long enough to hear me say, 'but in spite of all that you are more beautiful than I have ever seen you — except once.' " Jenny's heart pounded, but before she could reply, Jeff and Ann were at the clinic door. As usual, Ann was spotless in her uniform, every shimmering red hair aglow in the early morning sun. By contrast, Jenny felt plain and even more crumpled than her snatched nap had left her.

"How are they?" Jeff's voice was anxious in spite of Dr. Lance's reassuring smile, but when he stepped next to Twilight's bed and she opened her eyes, his worried look melted. In its place was pride, love, and something else so beautiful Jenny had to turn away. Jeff's eyes lit on his tiny son sleeping so peacefully in the little basket nearby, and his eyes filled with a strange, unaccustomed mist. Jenny admired this brother-in-law of hers more at that moment than ever before. Was there anything so touching as seeing a strong man who was not afraid to show emotion? She remembered discussing it once with Lance.

"It is a crime the way parents teach their children, 'little boys don't cry,' " he had said. "They grow up with this feeling and bottle everything inside. They have more heart attacks, high blood pressure, and ulcers — all because of that ridiculous idea that they mustn't cry or it will lessen their masculinity. If they could only realize what it is doing to their systems, they wouldn't be so precious about guarding their feelings."

"Do you ever cry?" Jenny had blurted out. Lance had had the grace to turn red.

"Not very often," he had admitted, then laughed, showing strong, white teeth. "I was raised in the 'little boys don't cry' school, too!"

Ann was touching Jenny gently on the shoulder. "Go home, Jenny. I can take over now. I had some rest."

Lance heartily seconded the motion. "I'll take you. Oh, Jeff, by the way, since the storm is all over, do you want the pilot with his bush plane to take Twilight into Chelan for a thorough going over?"

Jeff didn't hesitate. "What do you recommend?"

"I'd like to see her go. Even though we took every precaution, there's always the chance of unexpected infection."

Twilight's voice was surprisingly clear. "Infection wouldn't dare set in, but if Lance wants me to go, I will."

"Good girl!" he approved.

Jenny added, "Why can't I go with Ann so you can get started? By the time you get the pilot, we'll have Twilight ready. She came off in such a hurry that she didn't have time to bring much! We can get what's needed, then later Ann can open the clinic for first-aid help."

She was stopped short by Twilight's pleading eyes. "Can I take my baby?"

"You bet!" Dr. Lance was forceful. "I know you want to feed him yourself, not put him on a formula. Where you go, he goes." It didn't take long for the girls to get Twilight set up, and how gently Lance and Jeff carried the stretcher to the plane. Her smile was almost back to its old self as she waved. Lance and Jeff would accompany her, Jeff to remain in town for the few days she would be there and Lance to talk with the doctors.

Jenny felt curiously let down as she

watched the plane out of sight. She must be more tired than she knew. If she could have seen her own enormous eyes, as Ann did, she would have known what a strain the night had been.

Yet Ann rejoiced in what she saw in Jenny's eyes. She had never mentioned to anyone in Stehekin the brief time Jenny and Lance had known each other, or under what circumstances. Now she saw in Jenny's face the same look of love that had been on Twilight's and was glad. She had caught Lance's feelings weeks before and realized that for some reason he was holding back from Jenny. But Jenny's look reassured her. All was well, or would be in time, she added to herself with a chuckle. Now she was gentleness itself as she led Jenny to the wagon and drove her home.

Great fallen branches gave mute testimony to the havoc the storm had left in its wake. Ann, the irrepressible, couldn't help but blurt out, "They should have named him Thomas Jefferson Storm!"

Jenny giggled at the thought. Leave it to Ann! Nothing ever got her down.

She shot a curious, sidelong glance at her friend. "I wonder what Don Parker will have to say about the baby."

Ann blushed furiously. "He likes babies."

Jenny's eyebrows raised, but she was careful to keep her voice nonchalant. "Oh?"

Ann's color deepened. "We — that is — we just happened to be talking about Twilight and Jeff and their coming baby, and he said he liked babies."

They had reached Jenny's cabin by now. Ann refused to come in, saying she had grabbed a bite of breakfast earlier with Jeff. Jenny promised to drive over later with lunch for her. "I'll make it a picnic," she promised. "We can take it outside — it's still warm enough."

When Ann left, all Jenny wanted was a hot shower. She was glad they weren't like some of the valley families who had to pack water from the rushing creeks.

"I may be an outdoors girl, but the one thing I do appreciate is indoor plumbing!" She shivered at the thought, then laughed at her loud, emphatic remark. The needle spray of water revived her, and she toweled off briskly, intending to crawl in bed immediately. But when she had slipped the soft blue gown over her head, she found she was no longer sleepy. Touching off a small fire, she curled up close to it and stared into the flames.

What had caused this vibrant feeling of being really alive for the first time? Why did she tingle all over? Was it the effect of the hot shower followed by icy cold, or did it have something to do with the way Lance had raised her from the chair so demandingly the night before? If Jeff hadn't chosen that exact moment to enter, would she have really blurted out how much she had fallen in love with her husband? And what about when he returned?

He doesn't love me, she reminded herself, a lone tear squeezing itself out between her tightly closed lids. He married me to come to Stehekin and help the people and let his hand heal. Well, he had done both. The accident that just a year ago had crippled him, seemingly permanently, had faded into the past. Even the short time they had been in Stehekin had proven the worth of his decision. And what of hers? Yes, she told herself positively, if I hadn't married him, Twilight would have died last night. Even though the pilot is seldom grounded, he couldn't have flown her out of here last night.

I didn't know love could hurt so much. It was easier when we were just friends. But if he should learn to care? The question forced itself into her heart. It could be heaven. It could be the kind of marriage Mother and Dad shared for so long.

Restless, Jenny walked across the cabin floor, looking out into the autumn world. A mule deer had come to the old apple trees back of the place, and a dainty doe followed it. Two birds flew by, close together, the smaller following the larger. A pair of chipmunks raced across the front walk. Always two. Male and female, as God had created them. But only mankind knew the harshness and agonizing of unreturned love.

Yet was that entirely true? What of the defeated buck in the battle for a doe? What of the rejected bull moose, or any other animal? It was too much for Jenny's tired mind. She must relax, rest. Turning to the small desk, she took out pen and paper. While she waited for sleep to come, she might as well catch up on her correspondence. Page after page she filled, curled up in the big chair, letting the completed pages drift like white snowflakes to the bearskin rug on the floor. Time enough later to put them in the proper envelopes, which she also addressed and let slide to the floor. At last her tired pen ceased. The fire burned low and red, then went out. But Jenny slept, unaware of the passing time, oblivious to the fact that a hungry Ann waited for her lunch. Nature had been pushed too far; now it demanded she should rest.

The afternoon was far gone when the door opened quietly. Lance's heart bounded with joy as he saw the little figure asleep in the big chair. Very softly he stole across the room, intending to waken her and once and for all settle things by declaring his love. It need not make any difference to her if she didn't care, but somehow he felt that she did. The night before, and then this morning, he had seen a matching glow in her face that had not been there before.

Frowning at the crackling paper on the floor, he automatically caught the partly filled envelope that chose that moment to slip from her lap and join its counterparts on the rug. Without intending to, he noted the partially completed address:

Dr. Scofield
7782 Lake Washington Blvd.
Seattle

Scofield? Dr. Scofield? He knew no one of that name. Why should Jenny be writing to a Seattle doctor? A quick pang of alarm shot through him. Was something wrong that she didn't want to tell him? Without

104

thinking, he let his eyes drop to the final paragraph of her letter.

"You'll never know how dear you are to me, how much I appreciate everything you've done, and how I love you for it.

Always yours,
Jenny"

For a moment, Lance thought he was going to stop breathing from the sheer pain that went through him. Incredible! That just moments before he was to tell her of his own love, he should stumble across this evidence that she already cared for another. Was it possible this was only an old friend? Then why should she sign herself "Always yours"? No, she must love someone. Why had she lied to him, told him there was no one?

He thought back to the exact words the day he had asked her to marry him for the sake of Stehekin and her sister: "Are you engaged?" . . . "No. I'm too busy for that yet." He hadn't asked her if she loved someone else. Now he knew she did. What an unforeseen complication!

He wished he had not come home just then. Better not to know she cared for another. Yet was that really true? A mocking smile crossed his face.

Jenny stirred in her sleep, and quickly and noiselessly letting the betraying letter join its mates, Lance went back outside, this time entering with a great show of noise. Even in those few moments, he had made his decision. She was his wife; he would never let her go. But this time, she must come to him. The words of love that even at that moment trembled unsaid on his lips would be buried deep inside. He had her trust, her respect. And after all, he paraphrased to himself, "God's in His Heaven, and Dr. Scofield is far away!" With a slight smile on his lips, he banged into the cabin.

"Hey, Jenny, I'm home!" Not by a trace did he show the wound he had received a few minutes earlier, but neither, to Jenny's dismay, did he pursue the line of action that had begun the previous evening. At times during the rest of that day and the days that followed, he caught her looking at him when she did not know he could see her questioning gaze.

He couldn't quite make out what was coming until one evening after leaving the clinic she asked, almost too casually, "By the way, Lance, the night Twilight had her baby, you started to ask me something?"

He forced his own voice to calmness. "Good heavens, what a memory you have! Must not have been important, whatever it was." He had the satisfaction of seeing her lips droop with disappointment at his blunt answer. What does she expect? he demanded of himself, savagely, in order to keep from taking her in his arms. Does she think I'm going to fall for her charms after she lied to me? But she didn't lie, his conscience insisted. She only said she wasn't engaged.

He ignored the pointed little jabs of his own subconscious and deliberately changed the subject. "Won't be long until winter, will it?"

She seemed slow to respond, and when she did it was a rather inane remark about the falling leaves. She couldn't express herself even on the weather at that moment. She had been so sure Lance returned her love, but if he thought it hadn't been important, she knew where she stood.

As the days passed by into weeks, Lance became more and more remote in some ways. Evenings that they had planned to spend talking over the day's work in front of their fireplace were more often than not spent with him buried in a medical book and Jenny also with a book in her hands, but not turning the pages rapidly enough to convince him she was reading. Things at the clinic were slow now that the summer visitors had for the most part gone their own ways. When winter came, each of them realized, it would be even more difficult for them. Sometimes they might be snowed in for days.

I wouldn't care, Jenny thought passionately, if only Lance . . .

It wouldn't matter, Lance told himself bitterly, if Jenny cared. Then I would welcome the snow that would shut us in, all the rest of the world out.

The golden leaves lay in piles now, browning under the nippy nights and chill mornings. Gone was the friendly blue sky, replaced by an icy blue, warning them of the approaching season. Also gone were the great flocks of Canada geese who had winged their way south, filling the air with their honking farewells. Gone was the slow, easy Indian summer. People were getting prepared for the winter season. Even Ann had gone. There wasn't enough work to keep Jenny busy, let alone Ann. But Ann planned to come back for Christmas.

Everything is going away, Jenny thought,

watching the changing scene outside her little bedroom window. Everyone, too. Only the round-the-year residents are left. But there was one thing left that even Jenny was not aware of, the thing that was keeping Lance and her apart, and that was his memory of a white letter drifting to the floor and the name it conjured up with it, the name of Dr. Scofield. Lance had even built up a mental image of his rival, while out chopping wood and stacking it against the long winter ahead. He was probably thin and dapper, a dandy. Did he know how wonderful Jenny was? He shan't have her, Lance vowed. Am I a poor stick like Peter, Peter Pumpkin Eater, who couldn't keep his own wife?

If Jenny could have known his state of mind, surely she could have soothed his fears with a single word. But there was no way of knowing that the thing standing between her and her happiness was that innocent letter she had written to her old doctor friend in Seattle, who — though a fine surgeon — had taken care of her and Twilight from their childhood.

Chapter 7

"Jenny, come here, please." Lance's words were quiet, yet filled with excitement. He was standing on their little porch looking into the yard. Jenny slipped to his side, making a little O of her mouth. There stood three deer, their soft eyes unafraid, waiting for a handout. This in itself wasn't unusual. They had learned Dr. and Mrs. Reeves were always good for a treat. What was unusual was their appearance. The first snow of the season had begun to fall, and some of it sifted lightly on the deers' heads and backs.

"They're frosted!" Jenny's exclamation amused Lance, but he had to nod agreement. The beautiful animals *did* look as if they had just left a bakery where they had been dusted with fine sugar.

It amazed the two who had come from the city how beautiful not only the deer could be, but the entire world. Lance and Jenny were like two children, hurrying into outdoor-type clothing, pelting one another with snowballs. She was an expert at piling up supplies of hard, small snowballs and firing them with unerring accuracy. Lance wasn't so adept. In fear of being defeated, he at last rushed Jenny, ignoring her screams of excitement, washed her face with a big handful, and tossed her into a handy billow of nearby white.

"You miserable wretch!" She came up wet and shining. Gathering her defenses, she sent a volley of the small little snowballs after him as he took refuge just inside the kitchen door. There was release for both of them in getting outdoors. It was growing more and more difficult to maintain their aloofness to one another, each wondering if by some word or action he had betrayed himself to the other. Now Jenny rushed into the kitchen after Lance, heedless of the wet snow she was tracking. She was unprepared for the silence of the room, but when the door closed behind her, there he stood, laughing.

"You dared to wash my face," she announced, her ferocity somewhat diluted by the strand of wet hair that had escaped her stocking cap and hung in the middle of her forehead.

"There was a little girl, who had a little curl," he taunted her, dodging her pretended onslaught with a leftover roll from the counter. Ducking behind the table, he finished singsonging the rhyme, now adding variations the author had never intended:

"When she was good (which wasn't very often)

She was very, very good,

But when she was bad (which she is most of the time and right now!) . . ."

He left the safety of the table and ducked behind a chair, holding it in front of him as a lion tamer does, and adding triumphantly from his improvised shelter:

"Jennet Trevor Reeves was *h-o-r-r-i-d!*"

Helpless with laughter, Jenny collapsed into the chair and laughed until she cried. Seeing her so happy, Lance determined to break through the wall that had begun to grow between them,

"Pray tell me something, lady." He fell to his knees in a mock gesture of deep humility. "Prithee, what hast thou to offer a poor servant who is starving, a beggar as it were, your slave? A crust of bread? A sip of water? Or better yet" — he cast a wicked eye at the hot apple pie she had carefully removed from the oven shortly before the snowball fight — "A piece of pie?"

Wishing to answer in kind, Jenny searched the kitchen with a quick glance, looking for something she could use as a scepter. Grabbing a spatula, holding it aloft, she proclaimed in as haughty a manner as any royalty would command, "I dub thee Sir Snowball, to serve me long and faithfully, as long as we both shall live." Why had she quoted the words from the wedding service? she demanded of herself furiously, even as in the twinkling of an eye Lance's comedy turned to drama.

"As long as we both shall live, Jenny?" His tone suddenly became harsh, bitter. "But what about Dr. Scofield?"

"Dr. Scofield!" Jenny echoed, puzzled. What on earth did Dr. Scofield have to do with anything? And why did Lance speak of him in such an unpleasant way? He was being totally ridiculous — completely unreasonable. "What do you have against poor Dr. Scofield?" she demanded.

"Yes, poor Dr. Scofield! That day I came home from Chelan, the letter you were writing slipped to the floor. I couldn't help but see it."

"So what?" she said frostily.

Her coolness should have warned him, but he rushed on, forgetting the fun they had been having such a short time ago. "So how can you sit there, a married woman — even if you aren't really my wife — saying in that outraged tone of voice 'So what?' "

His mimicking of her words were perfect even to the inflection. They only added fuel to the fire.

She jerked free from the hands he had pinned to the sides of the chair, imprisoning her almost within the circle of his arms. In another moment she would have leaned forward and pleaded with him never to let her go. Instead she stood erect, defiant.

"So I have the misfortune at the moment to be your wife. Does that carry with it the privilege of your reading my mail and making unfounded accusations?" Her icy scorn triggered the temper he had held in check so long.

"It does when my wife writes and tells another man she loves him!" The gasp Jenny made was lost in his attack. "I thought after these months up here you were beginning to care about me! I thought we could make it the kind of marriage my parents shared and the kind you seem to want. But you" — he pointed his finger at her — "you just couldn't play the game, could you? You told me you were not engaged; why didn't you tell me you loved this Dr. Scofield? Why, Jenny, why?" By now he was almost thundering.

Jenny could only stammer, completely

caught off-guard, "Why should he make any difference to us?"

Lance's words of showing that he was learning to care had shaken her. A wild joy was spreading through her at a rushing pace, but he kept on and on about Dr. Scofield. "Make any difference? Tell me one thing, Jenny, do you love this Dr. Scofield?"

"Of course, I love Dr. Scofield." Jenny's demure answer stopped him in his tracks, but only for a moment. With blazing eyes, he seized her shoulders and shook her like a child.

"He will never have you, do you understand? You are mine, my wife, and you will stay that way!" By this time Jenny was as angry as he was.

She twisted from his grasp. The words poured out. "You beast!" She held out her arms, wincing a little. "There will be bruises on my shoulders where you grabbed me!"

Lance was too hurt and angry to care. "Then put these with them!" He crushed her close, turned her protesting face toward his, and effectively silenced her. Jenny could feel his heart pounding; her own kept time.

When he finally released her it was only

to ask with biting scorn, "Has your precious Dr. Scofield ever kissed you like that? Tell me, Jenny, has he?"

If he had thought to conquer her by force, he was mistaken. Not betraying by one movement how deeply his embrace had stirred her, she shot back, "No he hasn't, Mr. Lancelot Reeves." She fairly snapped the words. "Your insane jealousy has ruined everything! Just when I was beginning to think that *I* . . ." She broke off with a sob, but quickly gathered her dignity, her brown eyes pools of accusation.

"I suggest you go ask Twilight about Dr. Scofield. When she tells you the truth, which she will, I also suggest you come back here with a good strong apology for me!"

He glared at her. "Apologize for kissing my own wife? Never! But I will ask Twilight about this Dr. Scofield! Right now!" He strode out the door, slamming it hard behind him and startling the deer, who had bounded away during the snowball fight but had returned in time to cock their ears and hear the human quarrel going on.

"You don't need to look so wise," he shouted at them in passing. "If you could talk, you'd probably argue, too!" If Jenny hadn't been so upset, she would have shouted with laughter at the sight of the formal Dr. Lance Reeves taking out his anger by talking to wild animals! As it was, she sank down on the couch and had a good cry.

"I hate him!" The words filled the room with an ugly sound. "Why did he have to spoil things? If he can't trust me, what good is it that he's starting to care? What a jealous nature. I didn't dream he was like that." She refused to look at Lance's side of the picture. All she could see was his attack, unprovoked as it had been. Fresh tears sprang to her eyes. Everything was ruined now. How could they go on trying to be polite, with all this undercurrent between them?

By the time Lance had driven through the snow to Twilight and Jeff's, he had cooled down a bit. How awful he had been to shout at Jenny that way. How lovely she had looked even in her angry mood, even when she froze in disdain. What would he find out from Twilight? He hoped Jeff would be busy outside.

Luck favored him. Twilight had just put the baby to bed, and Jeff had gone into town for some supplies in case the snow fell steadily for some time.

It was hard to work the conversation

around to his question, Lance found. He finally maneuvered it by asking if Twilight missed her Seattle friends and then casually inserting, "What's Dr. Scofield like?"

He was surprised at the glow in Twilight's eyes. "He's a dear! Everyone loves him!" Lance's heart sank. Evidently his competition was worthy of Jenny's love. He still can't have her, Lance promised himself.

Twilight's face lit up with pleasure as she went on. "From the time I can remember, Dr. Scofield was always there. Even though he was a skilled surgeon, he continued with his family practice."

Funny, Lance thought, how old is the guy?

Twilight was on her feet. "I think I have a picture of him." She rummaged through a curiously carved chest in the corner and came up with a small bit of cardboard.

"This is Dr. Scofield with Jenny and me just before I came here the first time, but he really hasn't changed much."

Lance took a deep breath and reached for the picture. He wondered if he could stand to look at the man. When he did, he felt two inches tall. Jenny and Twilight were standing with their arms around a man, faces turned to him. The camera had faithfully recorded their devotion to the gray-haired, fatherly man who gazed directly into the lens. He was saintly looking; there was no other word to describe him. A lump the size of a baseball threatened to shut off Lance's windpipe. He had been jealous of their beloved family doctor!

Something of his stricken look pierced Twilight's chatter. "Why, whatever is the matter, Lance? Are you ill?"

He shook his head. "No, on the contrary, I am feeling much better." He grabbed his coat, mumbling that he had to get back to Jenny, and strode out, leaving Twilight puzzled, with the picture of Dr. Scofield still in her hands.

Why didn't Jenny tell me? his mind demanded. What chance did she have to tell you anything, you brute? his conscience answered. You saw a letter, one not intended for anyone but a good old family friend, and built what was almost a federal case out of it. You accused and threatened and stormed, all because you couldn't stand the thought of what you thought was deceit. And what has it gained you? The loss of her trust and perhaps her love, maybe forever.

By the time Lance reached the cabin,

Jenny had regained control and, pale but determined, was kneading bread on the big board. He stole in quietly, appearing in the doorway before she could hear him. The snow had completely muffled his approach. What a contrast between the pale girl before him, shadows in her eyes, and the one who had knighted him Sir Snowball in the moments of foolishness a little while before.

Something of his feelings showed in his voice. "Jenny." Her eyes widened and she took one step back. She's afraid of me, Lance realized. But a moment later, she continued with her kneading.

"It was inexcusable of me," he told the silent figure. His heart couldn't stop there. "Let's just say that I have learned to love, admire, respect you with all my heart. I couldn't stand to know you loved someone else. Forgive me, Jenny. It's because I love you so much that I acted as I did."

"But you didn't trust me." There was no inflection at all in her voice. She kept on kneading, not even looking up. Lance didn't know what to say, but she continued, her voice the same monotonous tone, no hint of her inner turmoil coloring the words with any emotion.

"We should never have married, Lance."

She ignored his unvoiced protest. "We took the marriage vows lightly, because of our own needs. We entered into what should have been a sacred relationship because I wanted medical help for Stehekin, and you needed to get away from pressure."

This time he could keep silent no longer. "Jenny, I loved you from the moment you defied me. Do you really think I would have married you if I hadn't cared? I banked on your sense of honor and the beauty of this place to help you come to love me."

She shook her head. "It's no good, Lance. I don't want to stay here any longer with you. Without trust, there is nothing. I knew today, when you slashed at me, you really hated me for what you thought I was. If there had been love instead of hate, you would have trusted me in spite of what appeared to be concrete evidence. But you didn't." She stopped working, this time looking squarely into the eyes of the man before her. The suffering she saw almost weakened her, but she stiffened her courage to do what must be done.

"I want to go away for a while, back to Seattle. I can stay with the Matthewsons and visit Dr. Scofield." There wasn't a hint of sarcasm in her voice. "He's the one who saved my life a few years ago with open-heart surgery. He knew I must have it in order to live a full life, and he insisted I go through with it. Love him? Of course I love him. He is part of my very life."

Lance made a choking sound. If he could only swallow his earlier words. Now he pleaded, "Jenny, if I had only known! Can't you forgive me? I forced you into such a hasty marriage, how could I know you didn't love someone else?"

"I have never loved any man enough to want to spend my life with him," she replied, eyes steady. "I was beginning to care for you, but your lack of trust in me has killed that. I want to go away."

"Stay, Jenny," Lance asked huskily. "Stay and let that love develop."

"It's too late." She turned away to wash her hands at the sink, unable to keep the tears of disappointment from showing. "I had begun to put you on a pedestal, making an idol of you. Now it's shattered." She laughed bitterly.

It was that little laugh that kept Lance from following her when she went into her own room, leaving the door open, and began to pack. She was right. It had been a shock for her. But if she had begun to look up to him, time away from him might be all in his favor. He would no longer oppose her going.

"Jenny." He lounged in the doorway. "There is no way I can take back the unforgivable words I threw at you. Yet when you are in Seattle looking out over the water, don't forget there's someone back here pleading, 'Come home, Nurse Jenny.' I'll be needing you, wanting you, loving you, not only while you're gone, but for always. We can still have that marriage you spoke of, two against the whole world, fighting together. But, Jenny, when you come home, and I pray to God that you will, I don't want a friend, I want a wife. To love, to honor, to cherish." His voice broke, and he turned on his heel and walked blindly out into the snow.

Jenny sat motionless on the edge of her bed. The timbre of his voice still hung in the room. To love, to honor, to cherish. Did he mean it? If only those other words had not been spoken! They steeled her determination. She had to get away. If she let herself be swayed now, she would never know whether it was real love on his part or remorse at having treated her so.

Hastily scribbling a note to Twilight to save explanations, Jenny finished packing.

Lance could take her to the boat dock before the snow got too deep. She would leave Stehekin for a time. The thought struck a pang into her heart. It would soon be Thanksgiving; she would miss it. The whole community had talked of sharing a harvest dinner; she wouldn't be here. But I'll be with the Matthewsons, she told herself, thrusting down the pang of parting.

If Lance had said one more word about her staying, on the way to the boat dock, it would have turned the trick. Already Jenny was having qualms about leaving. The snowy setting was superb. Great billows lined the road; branches dripped heavily to the ground with the weight of it. How could she bear to leave? But she must.

"Good-bye, my darling. Don't stay too long." Lance's whispered words remained with her on the entire trip down the lake to Chelan. Scalding tears, but tears that healed, flowed into Jenny's pillow that night. The next day she took up her cudgels of pride and gathered up her story. Ann would be waiting; she must not suspect the truth. Or . . . Would it be wrong to tell her? Ann had always known her marriage wasn't what it had seemed to be at the first.

With a quick decision, Jenny determined to tell her the whole thing. But it wasn't as easy as she had thought. Several days passed before the girls could get together.

When Ann asked, "And how is Lance?" Jenny was so keyed up, she burst into tears.

"I don't know, Ann, I don't know." It was quite a while before Jenny could get the story out. Ann sat round-eyed, listening.

When Jenny finished, all Ann could say was, "If I read this in a book, I'd throw the book aside as impossible! Things like this just don't happen in real life!" Her remark was exactly what Jenny needed.

"They do to me," she sobbed. "But, oh, Ann, what shall I do now?"

Ann was quiet for a long time, then she spoke.

"Do you love him, Jenny?" Her simple question dried her friend's tears.

"With all my heart."

"Then don't let pride stand in your way. He evidently cares for you a great deal, or he wouldn't have reacted so wildly when he thought your marriage was threatened. I know, you've told me your marriage was for convenience. By the way, I thought convenience marriages went out with the Dark Ages! But you didn't count on one

125

thing. Evidently Lance fell for you, and fell hard. You were dedicated to Twilight and obsessed by the thought of getting medical help for her and for the rest of Stehekin. But Dr. Lance? You can't tell me he would up and marry a strange girl who had blazed away at him in front of practically the entire hospital staff just for the sake of getting away to let his hand rest! I'm inclined to believe he told you the truth. Besides, no one could be in Stehekin long and not fall in love."

Quick as a flash, Jenny caught the significance of her words.

"You mean you . . ."

Ann nodded, her eyes soft with happiness. "I'm going back to Stehekin and will be a Christmas bride. Mrs. Don Parker!" She hugged her arms close, eyes closing in mock rapture. "Can't you just see my carrot top with that white veil? I'll mow the poor man down. He won't have a chance!" Abandoning her pose, she fixed a stern eye on Jenny.

"And you're going back with me! That's over a month away. You can use the excuse that I need you to help with my trousseau to stay away that long. But I have to have you as my matron of honor in a Christmas holly-berry red dress and that Golden

West Lodge decorated with spicy green fir, cones, and candles."

For an instant, Jenny was back in that same Golden West Lodge, standing with Twilight as she was married. A wave of homesickness went through her. Was Ann right? Did Lance love her? That was something she would have to decide before Christmas. And more important, was the love she had felt for him really stifled by his rude actions, or would it forgive and go on to flower?

Ann seemed to divine her thoughts. "Don't be afraid to believe, Jenny. Was he really any more ill-mannered to you than you were that day to him — and in front of everyone? He at least had the grace not to start a fight in the presence of a lot of big-eared witnesses!"

Jenny felt as if Ann had struck her. It was true! She had acted even more childishly that day in the hospital than Lance had a few days ago! Then weren't they even?

"I'll write him tonight!" she promised Ann, her eyes dancing.

Ann looked at her a little warily. "I would suggest you be careful what and how you write."

Jenny recalled her words later that night as she nibbled the end of a pen. Discarded

pages bore mute evidence that her letter
had not been as easy to write as she had
thought it would be. Finally she grinned to
herself impishly. Ann's words had straightened out her thinking. But she didn't want
Lance to know it quite yet. Instead, she
would revert back to her old friendliness
with Lance, then surprise him by accom-
panying Ann to Stehekin in time for
Christmas! Her face glowed as she bent to
the page and dashed off the note.

Dear Lancelot,
   Just a note to let you know I arrived
safely. Ann is well, and the Matthewsons send their love. I am not quite sure
just how long I will be staying. Ann is
getting married and wants me to help
with all the shopping, so will plan to do
that.
   Tell Twilight I will bring a surprise
for her and the baby when I come. I
would enjoy hearing from you — if you
have the time to write, that is.
                              Faithfully,
                              Jenny

There, if that didn't set him wondering,
nothing would! It was with a sigh of complete satisfaction that Jenny turned out her

light and slept, while in snowbound Stehekin a young doctor paced the floor, regretting his hasty actions and wondering if she would ever come back.

Chapter 8

If Jenny had hoped to bring her errant husband back in line with the cryptic letter she sent him, she was to be sadly disappointed. She watched patiently for an answer, reminding herself that now that winter had set in, there were only three mail boats a week to Stehekin. When it came, it was short and to the point.

Dear Jenny,

It was nice to hear from you. Surprisingly, for winter time in Stehekin, I have been extremely busy. By the way, did you know that your name Jenny is a derivative of the Olde English Guinevere? Don't forget what happened to her. As long as you call me Lancelot, perhaps I'll call you Guinevere.

And it was signed, of all things, "Lancelot Reeves, M.D."!

Jenny's face burned. What did he mean by his remarks? That Guinevere had fallen in love with Lancelot? Or did he refer to all the trouble she had stirred up with her unpredictable actions? Whatever he meant, it was clear he did not intend to let her get the best of him. Her first impulse was to dash off a hasty answer, then she checked herself, smiling slowly. Let him wait for her reply. He would see just how determined she could be! Unfortunately for her own little declaration of independence, she couldn't resist tucking his note under her pillow that night, undoing, at least in her own mind, all her staunch defiance of lord and master Lancelot Reeves.

Thanksgiving Day was hard for Jenny, in Seattle. The Matthewsons were away for the day. It had been all she could do to restrain herself from going back to Stehekin and her family and friends. Only the thought that Ann, with whom she spent the day, was just as lonely for Stehekin and her own fiance cheered the despondent girl.

"Misery loves company," Ann told her, misty eyed. Jenny laughed. Ann was right. They had been moping around like two calves who had strayed from their mothers.

"Let's dress up and go out," Jenny challenged.

Ann perked up right away. Before long they had called in a reservation and were being seated in the plush dining room of one of Seattle's finest hotels, which had thoughtfully remained open for the holiday. It was fun to look at their surrounding neighbors to see who went out for dinner on holidays, besides themselves. Jenny's eyes rested on the face of a familiar older man nearby.

"Dr. Scofield!" she squealed, hurrying to his table.

The doctor's face lit up with pleasure. He had been resigned to spending Thanksgiving at a lonely dinner. Since his wife of many years had died, he usually attempted to work holidays. But this year he had been scheduled for an especially difficult piece of surgery the next day, so had taken this one off to rest. He wasn't as young as he had once been. Perhaps he should retire and let one of the younger men take over. But what of his still-active brain and medical skill? Some of these thoughts had been idly crossing his mind when Jenny called out.

Rising to meet her and her friend, he beckoned the waiter to bring extra chairs to his table.

"Yes," he insisted. "You must be my guests for dinner." Jenny was one of his favorite people, and he had met Ann several times before. In fact, she had even worked with him on occasion.

"Now, tell me all about yourself, Jenny. How's that talented young husband of yours? I've heard about him from some of my colleagues at the hospital. Isn't he here?" He looked around anxiously, as if expecting Lance to appear at any moment. Jenny had the grace to blush, but not by the movement of a hair did she indicate her embarrassment.

"I'm down helping Ann select her trousseau," she said coolly, although the fork with which she was delicately cutting her salad trembled a bit. But Dr. Scofield was too happy to see her to notice; only Ann caught the little movement and smiled to herself.

Throughout the beautifully served dinner, traditionally Thanksgiving from the turkey to the pumpkin pie, they chatted. Dr. Scofield beamed at the two beautiful young ladies who had become his unexpected guests, banishing loneliness at least for a time.

"You know," he said slowly, fingers drumming on the white tablecloth. "I would like to see your Stehekin sometime. It sounds like a place that might appeal to an old codger like me when I retire."

"Retire!" The two girls' eyes were round. "Dr. Scofield, you are planning to retire?"

"Well, not today or tomorrow," he laughed. "But one of these days I just might. By the way, how would Lance like to replace me as head surgeon? With his returned skill, I'm sure he would get top consideration for the post."

Jenny was still for so long that the doctor wondered if she had misunderstood him in some way. When she spoke, it was in sober tones. "I don't know. Stehekin needs him so badly. Yet . . ."

Her voice trailed off as Ann quietly finished the sentence, "Yet his surgical skill will not be used very much there."

Dr. Scofield was sorry for the shadow he had cast on their pleasant afternoon. "I may not retire for years," he hastily amended, but Jenny's face didn't lighten. When they had arranged the marriage, she and Lance hadn't looked that far into the future. They had only discussed the immediate need of Stehekin and of his hand that needed to heal. Now Dr. Scofield's remarks had brought up all kinds of questions. It was true that Lance would never be able to use his skill to its utmost in Stehekin. He was a genius with a scalpel. But if he left Stehekin . . . Jenny refused to even consider the thought. Time enough for it when he brought it up. She wasn't going to cross bridges that might never be built, especially here, with Dr. Scofield and Ann looking at her so anxiously.

"Jenny." Dr. Scofield had her full attention now. There was no time for mind wandering. "If you are going to stay until just before Christmas, would you consider doing some specialing at the hospital? The usual run of winter flu has left us terribly shorthanded, and then with the increase in accidents from wet pavements and so forth, we can certainly use you. What about coming back for the next few weeks and helping out?"

Jenny's eyes sparkled. Not for the world would she admit that, even in the short time since she had left Stehekin, she had been bored to death, with nothing to do for hours on end when Ann was working. It was fine when they were off and shopping, planning for the wedding, but Ann had to keep up with her work.

"I'd love to!" Genuine appreciation of the offer underscored every word, and when Dr. Scofield dropped the girls off later, it was with the understanding that she would come in the next day and get her assignment from her old friend, the director of nurses.

"I hadn't realized that Dr. Scofield was head surgeon," Ann exclaimed. "Of course, I knew he was a fine surgeon, but he was always so devoted to his old family practice — how did he get that spot at the hospital?"

Jenny shook her head. She had been surprised also. To think, that he had left his own family practice and was now the surgeon most looked up to in the entire hospital!

"How did you keep from knowing?" Jenny wondered aloud.

Ann reminded her, "I spent all that time in Stehekin. Then, since I've been back, I decided to be on a sort of call register instead of sticking to one place. Most of my work has been with private patients, and the work I have done with him was in relation to aftercare. How could I suspect?"

"I guess you couldn't," she admitted. Then in a small voice, Jenny asked, "Ann?"

Her friend divined the thought before it was spoken. "I don't know what you're going to do about Lance. I know you love him and when you get through punishing him for his attitude, you'll go wherever he goes. But then just where does that leave

Stehekin? Of course, I'll be there, and really, Jenny, before you married Dr. Lance that was what you had counted on, wasn't it, a nurse in the community who could take care of smaller things?"

"Yes, but it has been so wonderful having a full-time doctor there."

Perhaps it was a touch of homesickness along with her concern for the future that caused Jenny to write the first really long letter to Lance that she had written since leaving Stehekin. She was so caught up with her own feelings and uncertainty that she didn't realize the impact her written words would have on him.

But Lance felt as if he had been struck when he read her letter a few days later. He had spent Thanksgiving with Twilight and the others, enjoying the friendly acceptance that was in their home. The baby was growing daily, Jeff and Twilight were more in love than ever, and as for Jingles and Aunt Lucy! Never since boyhood days had Lance cared for people the way he did them. They were special, real, people. They accepted without comment the fact that Jenny was staying on to help Ann with her trousseau. If there were any doubts of Lance's rather elaborate explanations, they weren't allowed to mar the holiday. Tommy and Honey, now Lance's devoted slaves, were in seventh heaven at having him around for a whole day!

So in spite of the ever-present ache within at the empty log cabin when he went home each night, he had been in good spirits. He could chop wood for hours now without any trouble from his hand. He could hold a scalpel surely and steadily, and when there was free time he spent it in whittling. Crude though his efforts were, they provided him extra practice in using that hand in a smaller way.

"Letter from Jenny," the friendly voice called even before the combination storekeeper and postmaster handed it over. "Nice thick one, too!"

Lance couldn't take offense at the words. Once he would have thought them the height of nosy impertinence. Now they were a symbol of sharing, of being glad for one who got a long-awaited letter in the snowbound stillness that was Stehekin.

Lance had fallen into the habit of meeting the mailboat, as everyone else did. It was a social time, as well as business. Waiting for the mail to be distributed was a choice time to catch up on all the news. This morning was no exception. In the space of thirty minutes, Lance found out how more of his patients were doing than three hours of telephone calling would have accomplished back in the city! These people really cared for one another, and if one didn't know how a certain family was getting on, someone else did. They kept track of their own. It was part of survival in this rugged country. If someone was to have an accident and not be found immediately, it could become tragedy.

Was there any place else on earth exactly like Stehekin? Lance couldn't help but wonder, as he had wondered many times. It really was unique. He wouldn't trade his experiences here for anything. They had shown him there were still people who had concern for something other than money and their own welfare.

All the way home, Jenny's letter felt warm against Lance's heart, where he had buttoned it into the pocket under his heavy parka. But fifteen minutes or so later he felt as cold as the burned-out embers in the fireplace, where his carefully banked fire had gone out while he dallied in the store, getting news. The first part had been of Thanksgiving Day with Ann and Dr. Scofield, and a pang had shot through Lance at the remembrance of his reaction to Dr. Scofield. Would she ever forgive him? The next few sentences showed that evidently she had not, at least not yet. He reread them, although they had burned into his mind with red hot brands, and there was no need to read them again. He knew them by heart already.

". . . and so I am going to be working at the hospital. They are terribly short-handed, and Dr. Scofield says I am desperately needed. I can be of real service . . ."

Where Jenny had been referring to a temporary job, Lance took it as permanent. She had made no mention of the fact that it would only be until Ann's wedding. She hadn't even thought of it. And all he could see was that she had found a job. She wouldn't be back.

For a moment he was tempted to rush back to the boat landing and go after her. Didn't he desperately need her, more than anyone else in the world possibly could? He groaned, thinking how she had just begun to trust and care for him, and he, clumsy oaf that he was, had crushed out that trust and caring by his own jealousy, as effectively as a heavy boot crushed the life from a tiny wild geranium! And unfounded jealousy, at that!

What should he do? Should he go? Yet he remembered how he had seen the shine in Jenny's eyes at knowing there would be adequate medical help in her beloved country. Determination steeled his eyes. He would stay. He would be all that she wanted him to be. In time, surely, she would forgive, but for now, he could not go. And he could not answer her letter. What could he say? He wasn't going to congratulate her on her job, and he had decided not to urge her to come home, so what was there left to write? All night long he wrestled with his problem, little heeding the soft snow that continued to fall, blanketing the world with its soft mantle of purest white.

Morning came. With it came hope. How could the world be so beautiful if Jenny was not coming back? It just couldn't, he decided. Even the dazzling blue sky above the towering, snow-laden firs would surely be dimmed if she decided to stay away. Although he didn't write, his heart went across the miles with its silent message, imploring, Come home, Jenny, come home.

The days passed slowly. Twilight, on the

rare occasions when she now saw Lance, was startled at the change in him. He had always been mature, but there had still been a certain boyishness in him. Now it was gone. He was all man, and the shadow in his eyes told her the winter hardships of Stehekin had not put it there. She mentioned it in her letters to Jenny, not wishing to pry, yet concerned about him.

"I don't know what's wrong with Lance," she wrote. "He is so quiet, so lacking in the magnetism that makes up his personality. It is as if the fire has gone out. I don't know what's bothering him, Jenny, but I'm glad you'll be home in another week or so. He needs you. And you need to come home. You've been gone too long."

Jenny wondered when she got that letter. It had been a long time since Lance had written her. Right then, she was too tired to think about it. As Dr. Scofield had said, they were quite shorthanded at the hospital. She was run off her feet in the children's ward, where she had been assigned, yet she was glad to do it. There was little time for personal worries now. When she got home it was only to throw herself into bed and rest until time for another shift.

She and Ann had different hours right now, so even her companionship was denied. Jenny had slipped into the routine of the night nurse, sleeping days, working the long, dark hours, and it was a time of unreality for her, after the clear, bright days of Stehekin. Had she dreamed them, or was this present life but a dream, from which she would presently awaken and find herself back in her own room in Aunt Lucy's "honeymoon cottage"? Would it become that for her? Lance had made it clear that if she returned it would be as a wife, not a good friend, or would she become both? That was something else she was too tired to consider.

And then it was over. Her last night of duty was completed; Ann's last assignment was finished. Their clothes were packed. All of Ann's carefully stored possessions were shipped, and the girls were back in Chelan for the night, awaiting the morning mailboat to Stehekin!

If the heavens themselves had decided to welcome those two nurses home, they couldn't have joined forces to produce a more glorious day. The fifty-five-mile-long Lake Chelan, which never froze, was as calm as a summer day. The banks of the lake were snow covered, with immense mountains rearing their white heads above.

Some of the snow was off the limbs of the green trees on shore, providing a study in green and white and the varying blues of lake and sky, and over it all poured the winter sun. Sickly it might look to those who spent winters in Florida, or California. To Jenny and Ann, tired from their extra efforts in the last hectic weeks, it looked like a beaming orb of approval.

"Does he know you are coming?" Ann's question broke the reverie of the two girls who, warmly clad, had been standing outside as the boat slowly made its way up the lake.

"No." The monosyllable was flat, and Ann didn't push farther. Yet she suspected something of what Jenny must be feeling. Her own heart, swelling with happiness of knowing that Don Parker, soon to be her bridegroom, was waiting for her, could still expand with compassion for Jenny. She couldn't bear to see the droop of unhappiness in Jenny's lips. Could Lance's feelings have changed? There had been no letter from him since Thanksgiving. Was he sick?

While her mind was racing, Jenny's was dully trying to accept the fact that perhaps her homecoming would not be what she had expected. She remembered Twilight's words, "You've been gone too long." Had

Lance changed? Some of the beautiful day dimmed at the thought.

"Let's go inside," she told Ann abruptly. "It's cold out here." Ann made no protest. She could see Jenny was very near the breaking point. In fact, if it hadn't been for the wedding, Ann wasn't sure Jenny would even have come home! Shaking her head in silent sympathy, she followed Jenny to their seats.

With the fickleness of nature, by the time they reached the boat landing at Stehekin, it had begun to snow again. Not the soft, beautiful kind, but hard, biting pellets of snow. They blinded the girls as they stepped ashore, Ann to be caught into the waiting arms of the muscular Don. Jenny stood alone, peering through the snow. Why hadn't she told someone she was coming, at least Twilight? Jeff could have come for her. Bitter tears, as frozen as the little snowflakes, joined their brothers and sisters on the ground. Why had she come at all?

"Over here." Someone hard and strong was leading her to a snow cat, settling her in it, and starting away from the dock. Lance's voice was as grim as the day. He had known Ann was coming today and, hoping against hope, had come to the landing. Would Jenny be with her? She had looked so small, so forlorn, as she stood there in the increasing storm. It had taken every bit of iron self-control he had to keep from picking her up bodily and depositing her in the snow cat. His jaw was set as he drove home. Had she just come for the wedding? She was here. Would she stay?

She'll stay, he told himself savagely. I can't let her go.

Does he want me? Jenny was asking herself. He is so cold, so aloof. I'm here, but will I stay? I have to, her heart cried, this is home. Anywhere he is will be home for me.

Two people at cross purposes. Two people at a crossroads. Two people, unable to read each other's thoughts, thoughts that ran on parallel tracks.

When they reached the cottage, Lance grabbed Jenny's hand and helped her up the path to the porch. It was fortunate they were both dressed warmly, for when they reached the front door he stopped her. He barred the door with his arm.

"Well?" His voice was stern. It was not the weather that made Jenny shiver miserably.

"Well, what?"

146

"You've come back, have you."

Hoping to crash through his barrier of reserve, Jenny blazed away angrily, ignoring the pain inside, "I'm here, aren't I?" She might as well have shouted at the giant snow-covered fir in the front yard for all the impression she made.

"And just why did you come?" His words, cold as the icicles hanging from the eaves, fell into Jenny's heart, stifling the eager things she had planned to tell him, the discoveries she had made about that same heart while she had been gone.

Dully she answered, "I came . . . I came . . ."

"Yes?" There was all the warmth of a snowman in his question.

"I have fallen in love —" Before she could complete the sentence, Lance's quick temper again betrayed him in a crucial moment.

"And you had the gall to come back and tell me that?"

In that moment, Jenny hated him with all her heart. If he had let her finish the sentence, she would have told him it was he who she had fallen in love with, but the hardness in his eyes whipped up her own anger. This was not the man she had come to love. This was a cold-eyed stranger, dictating terms, uncaring about her feelings. From somewhere far away came a voice that said, "With another man." In an instant, Jenny clapped her hand to her mouth. What had she done? It was true the man before her was not the Dr. Lance she loved, but what had possessed her to say such a terrible thing?

For a moment, Lance just stared at her. Then he picked her up and kicked open the door, striding through it purposefully and depositing her, dripping, on the floor inside. Catching her breath, unable to look at the stern man before her, Jenny subconsciously noted everything was just as she had left it.

"And I suppose next you'll be telling me you want to be this other man's wife!"

"Yes!" The involuntary cry rose from deep within Jenny, her longing proclaimed in the single word. Lance could not doubt her sincerity. Yet there was no way he could know it was he himself she referred to — he, blind man, who so insensitively rushed in where angels would have trod softly!

"You can get it out of your head." He said it very quietly, but his tone was deadly. "I will never give you a divorce. You will stay here with me." Without thinking,

Jenny's eyes wandered to the bedroom door behind which still lay most of her possessions. He intercepted the glance and laughed bitterly.

"Oh, you needn't worry. I still don't want a wife without love. You will be perfectly safe and left alone. I won't bother you." He started toward the door.

"Just don't think you can throw me over for anyone else. I'll keep you here forever before letting another man take my wife!"

Chapter 9

Was there ever a bride as beautiful as Ann? Don Parker thought not. As he and Lance stood before the banked altar of evergreens, softly lit by candles from a myriad of gleaming candlesticks, highlighting the red carnations and roses flown in for the wedding, his heart swelled with pride. Ann was beautiful. Her tall, graceful figure in the misty white, her crown of auburn hair, the glow in her eyes — she was lovely.

There had been no time for even whispered confidences between her and Jenny, so Ann had failed to note the proud way Jenny held her head and the look of deep sadness in her eyes. Not for anything would Jenny tell Ann on her wedding day that her own homecoming had been the worst day of her entire life. Sometimes . . . No, Jenny resolved. If that's the way he wants it, that's the way it will be. I married him for better or worse. I'm not heading for the divorce courts just because things are rough. Now she lifted her chin even higher and managed to smile as she walked down the aisle of the old Golden West Lodge.

Was there ever a woman as desirable as Jenny? Dr. Lance Reeves's eyes reflected the misery so carefully concealed in Jenny's own. Usually, he was adept at dropping a mask over his eyes; he had learned to disguise inner turmoil in his years in medicine. But not today. For that small figure in holly-berry red seemed etched indelibly on his heart. Why? Why had he driven her away, let her find someone else? It was well the congregation was too preoccupied to study him closely. Good old Dr. Scofield did see the look in Lance's eyes when Jenny first appeared, though, and he wondered. And Twilight had noticed something, too.

The church was beautiful. Outside, the snow had fallen until late afternoon, then given way to a brilliant moon on the winter scene. Even now, it shone through one of the windows, highlighting the deep, white snow that stood on each outside sill. It looked like a storybook church. Green everywhere. Red tapers. Shining silver bowls filled with Christmas flowers, sparkling in the candlelight. And the happiness! Happiness which touched every person present — except Jenny and Lance

— as the white-haired minister began.

"Dearly beloved, we are gathered here . . ." Muted voices. Ringing responses. To Jenny it was like a long-remembered dream. She found herself bitterly repeating the words, "In sickness, in health, for better or for worse, till death do us part."

And when Ann and Don responded, "I do . . . I will," Jenny and Lance carefully looked away from each other resenting the age-old words that could be the key to a lifetime of fulfillment but had only brought misery to them.

At last it was over, the unbearable strain of laughing, pretending all was well. The last cup of hot, spicy punch had been drunk. The last good wish, the last hasty hug, then Don and Ann were climbing into their chained station wagon for the short drive home.

They were honeymooning right there in Stehekin. Ann had said, practically, "With all that snow, we'll be completely isolated anyway, why go off somewhere to be alone?"

Don, who adored her, had been even more impressed by her lack of desire for an expensive stay in some commercial place. Now he looked down at her. Jenny had helped Ann get her trailing white wedding dress safely tucked in, and only she caught the words, "All right, wife, let's go home."

A sympathetic tear stung Jenny's eyes at the love and pride of possession in the first use of the word "wife" by Don. Would Lance ever call her that? she wondered. Small chance. She would be wife in name only. All the love and tenderness that had begun to grow seemed buried as deep as the earth beneath its white blanket of snow.

As she turned back to her own estranged husband, her pride made her even more beautiful than before. There he stood, tall, commanding, arrogant. She could only find coldness and censure in his face, not the least trace of approval or love. Why did life have to be so hard, anyway? Was this her punishment for marrying without love? Lifting her head haughtily, she brushed past him in silence for the long drive home.

Stehekin was at its height in beauty. Long, dark branches of trees were bent to the ground by the weight of their unaccustomed crystal burden. The sky was brilliant, with a happy moon riding high above and stars peeking out here and there from behind a stubborn cloud still trying to gather its neighbors for another onslaught on the earth below. The mountains gleamed.

Without thinking, Jenny blurted out, "If every man who covets could see this, war would cease."

The temperature in the car dropped another dozen points, and Lance's voice was freezing. "Would it?" Too late, she realized he had taken her remark personally. It was an effective silencer on conversation. After that, any further words would have been superfluous.

Dr. Scofield was staying with Twilight, Jeff, and baby Thomas Jefferson — whose name was now affectionately shortened to Tommy Two to avoid confusion with Aunt Lucy and Jingles's Tommy. The doctor was in his element. He had arranged to take some time off from the Seattle hospital, despite protest.

"I'm tired," he had argued, then added, with a twinkle in his eye, "If you don't give me some time off, I might just up and retire!" His request was honored immediately. His skill was too highly sought to risk losing for any cause. He had never threatened it before, but now the hospital buzzed with his comment. In faraway Stehekin, he neither knew nor cared. What a country!

"I'd be happy here the rest of my life," he confided to Lance after the first day in the clinic. He and Lance had become quite friendly.

Lance looked at him in surprise. "What of your responsibilities to the hospital?"

"They'd find someone else."

Lance cocked an eye at him. "Methinks I smell a rat. Just whom would they find as chief surgeon for such a big institution?"

"You."

"Me!" Lance's shock showed on his face. "I already have a job." He waved around the compact room. It didn't impress Dr. Scofield.

"I know. I was thinking of trading with you, at least for a while." Lance only stared. Trade with him? Take Dr. Scofield's position as head surgeon of such a large hospital? For a moment, his eyes gleamed. What a chance! The light faded.

"I don't know what Jenny would say."

Dr. Scofield had the grace to look a little ashamed. "I already told her what I had in mind." He squirmed uncomfortably, remembering Jenny's reaction on Thanksgiving Day when it had been discussed. "But I didn't tell her I would like to come here," he clarified. Again Lance could only stare, his mind whirling. Like Jenny, he had never really considered the future. He flexed the healed left hand, so supple and ready for a scalpel again. Yet now that he and Jenny were so at odds, he couldn't ask her to leave the land she had longed for the entire four years of her nurse's training. The land she had even married for, without love. A pang shot through him.

"Think about it," Dr. Scofield advised craftily. "Talk it over with Jenny."

That evening, curled before the blazing fire of her dreams with her silent, morose husband opposite, Jenny was startled by Lance's urgent voice. It was harsh, demanding.

"Jenny, would you ever want to go back to Seattle?"

She lay aside her mending, her hands still, her eyes large. What was coming next? "Why, I don't know," she stammered.

"Dr. Scofield wants to come here, at least for a while. He asked if I'd consider taking his post." Lance swung to face her squarely.

In a flash Jenny saw what it would mean to him. Stifling a half sob, she said, "Whither thou goest . . ." Once again, it was the wrong thing to say.

"You don't need to be sarcastic! I just want a straight answer out of you. Would you ever consider it, especially now that you love another man?" Jealousy colored the taunt he had resolved never to throw at her.

Something deep within Jenny rang a little bell. At least he cared enough about her to be jealous! She pushed the thought aside, and her answer was cool, clipped. "I suppose one place is as good as another . . . under the circumstances."

Only his iron self-control kept Lance from shaking her until she collapsed in his arms, where he wanted her so much. She was maddening, that's what she was, maddening! Deliberately, he walked to the window and looked out, little seeing the outside scene.

"It would mean a lot. My reputation would be established. But, of course, it's just wistful thinking. In the first place, it probably would never even be considered. Dr. Scofield has a crazy idea in his head that we could swap jobs. He'd be in Stehekin winters, we'd be in Seattle. Summers we would trade. That way, we would be here during the busy season. I doubt the hospital will even consider such a proposition. It seems utterly ridiculous to think they would. Yet he is respected . . ." As he turned away from the window, his voice trailed off, showing how very much he would like to try the plan, strange as it might seem.

Jenny swung around to face him. Their whole future hung in the balance. What she said now would make a difference forever, she realized. For a long time she stared at him, as he stood backed against the window. Her mind whirled. She mustn't make a mistake here. It was too vital. Closing her eyes for a moment for guidance, she managed to still the wild beating of her heart. If she acceded to his wishes, in time would he not at least respect her for it, even if he didn't love her anymore? She knew part of the reason Dr. Scofield had made such a preposterous suggestion was because of her own friendship with him. If Dr. Scofield knew Jenny and Lance weren't the happily married couple they appeared to be . . . She refused to consider it.

"That means we'd still be here part time. Why didn't you say so sooner? Men always hold back the good part until last." Her words were a triumph of will over emotion. "It will give me a chance to get some further practice on cases we don't get here. I've wanted to get in more work with children. There will be a real opportunity for me there, too."

"You'll go?" The dawning of the first human look that had appeared on Lance's face in regard to her since she came back almost undid her studied casualness.

"Of course. Our skills are needed in both places."

Dr. Scofield was delighted when they told him the next day. He promised to write the hospital, or better yet, as soon as he went back he would talk with them in person and arrange it, if they would approve the highly unusual request. In the meantime, he expected to enlarge on his remaining vacation in Stehekin by following Lance everywhere and learning the people's names and backgrounds.

The weather had continued to hold. But the day before Dr. Scofield was scheduled to leave, Stehekin dawned cloudy and gray. Jenny had a slight cold, and Lance ordered her to stay home.

"The clinic's trade has been slow. Dr. Scofield and I can handle it. Then, too, Ann is close. If anything comes up, we can get her."

Finally Jenny agreed, although her sniffles were so slight she didn't think they would really matter. Yet it was nice to be inside. She spent the morning curled up under a warm blanket, busily planning how she could make even an apartment in Seattle some kind of home while they were there. Her eyes snapped; her cheeks were red. Maybe Lance would like to rent the big apartment she and Twilight had lived in so long, the second floor of the Matthewsons'!

By afternoon she felt better and almost went over to the clinic. There was a strange foreboding in the air. The sky was leaden, and it was starting to snow again. She was probably just restless because of the depressing look outside. The atmosphere held a curious stillness, as a lull before a storm. Deciding she was letting her nerves get the best of her, she decided to make some pies. The community was having a shivaree for Don and Ann that night. All the women would bring dessert.

She had been unfamiliar with the custom before coming to Stehekin. Seems everyone waited until the newlyweds were asleep, then came in a group, tooting horns, banging pans, anything to make noise, and made the couple get up and let them in for a party. She giggled at the thought of Ann's face. Some of these country customs she had only learned recently herself were really fun.

"I'm going to make prune pies," she declared to the well-stocked woodbox in the kitchen. Getting out her materials, she smiled reminiscently. She remembered a day long ago when Mrs. Matthewson had told her and Twilight there would be prune pies for dessert.

"Prune pies?" they echoed simultaneously, not daring to look at one another.

"Oh, yes," the good woman had reassured them. "They are delicious."

The two girls had been polite but apprehensive. They needn't have been. Mrs. Matthewson had made her dough for the tender, flaky, double crusts the same as for apple or berry. Lining the pans with the dough, she added fresh, halved prunes that had been tossed with a mixture of sugar, cinnamon, and flour. Dotting this with butter, she carefully added the top crust and finished it off with a moistening of cream and a sprinkling of sugar. They were delectable! The Matthewsons liked them hot, but the girls preferred them after they had cooled down a bit. The flavor was better at a temperature not cold, not hot, but in between.

Now Jenny hummed happily as she finished three pies and got them in the oven.

Over the years she had learned to duplicate Mrs. Matthewson's masterworks, and in a short time three bubbling, delicately browned pies stood waiting on the sideboard.

The hours had gone by while she worked, and it was with a start of surprise she realized it was after five o'clock and the world outside had grown pitch black. That's funny, she thought, Lance had promised to be home at four. Oh, well, he must have had a last-minute call. Again her earlier depression fell over her like an enveloping blanket. In desperation, she turned on every light in the house and stoked the fireplace until its heat threatened to drive her out of the house.

Six o'clock came. With a determined tilt of her head, she jerked open the closet door and began to get out her outdoor clothes. She was going to the clinic to find Lance! There was a hard, cold knot of fear inside. Surely something must be wrong. He was never this late. Tying the strings of her hood, she was ready to go out the door when a vehicle drove in.

"Thank God he's home!" Jenny spoke aloud as she ran to the door to welcome her truant husband, the fear subsiding within her.

But it wasn't Lance who climbed out of the heavily snow-clad jeep; it was Jeff. The look on his face sent Jenny's newly restored peace of mind shattering into fragments.

"What is it?" She clutched Jeff's coat the minute he gained the porch and pulled him inside, dripping on the mat.

"It's all right, Jenny, don't worry." Jeff's steady hand gripped her.

"But where's Lance?" She was almost frantic.

Jeff held her shoulders in a tight grasp to steady her. "We're going to find him now."

"Find him! He's lost?"

"Not exactly." He forced the white-faced girl into a kitchen chair and pulled up one for himself, neither of them heeding the steady flow of melting snow that dripped into spreading pools on the floor.

"This afternoon one of the Baker men reported seeing smoke in that old log cabin up at the far end of the valley, off on that old road that is little more than a trail. A tenderfoot to Stehekin has decided to see if he could 'tough out' the winters here. It was too far away and across a valley for the man to see much, but he also reported a red flag waving above the cabin — a distress signal, he thought."

163

Jenny was in a fever of impatience. What did some tenderfoot have to do with Lance?

"Seems Baker came and told Lance, and Lance and Dr. Scofield took the snow cat and went out to investigate. The going was pretty rough, but they made it." Jeff stopped to chuckle, even though his face belied the sound.

"The red 'distress' signal turned out to be the man's long johns getting freeze dried! There was no one home. The man must have left his fire banked and come into Stehekin. The old jeep he used wasn't around his cabin, either. But as Lance and Dr. Scofield were coming back out, the tenderfoot's dog rushed them. He had been trained as a watchdog. He sprang directly at Dr. Scofield, but Lance stepped in between them. The dog barely grazed his arm" — Jeff ignored Jenny's groan — "but it threw Lance off balance. He fell hard against the side of the cabin."

"Go on." Jenny felt she had screamed the words.

"Dr. Scofield said Lance just crumpled up when he hit the cabin. A long log had been left sticking out of the old building, and his back had jammed against it. Dr. Scofield managed to get Lance inside where it was warm, but it was impossible to tell exactly how badly he was hurt. His back didn't appear to be broken, yet there might be internal injuries. At first he thought he would just stay with Lance, but he realized that when Lance recovered complete consciousness, he was going to be in some pretty bad pain and need more than what he had with him. He pinned a big note to Lance's blanket, where he'd see it first off when he came to, dashed out to the snow cat, which he had never run before, by sheer perversity got it started, and drove to the clinic as fast as he could. Ann was on her porch as he went by. He stopped just to tell her what happened, but she made him wait for her to grab warm clothing and leave a note for Don to get in touch with me, and they went back."

Jenny's eyes were filled with fear. Had she come back to Lance only to lose him so soon? Closing her eyes against the pain, she asked, "How long ago was that?"

"Ann 'dated' the note about four o'clock."

Jenny moaned, then pulled herself together. "But it's after six!"

"Don didn't get home until just a little while ago. As soon as he did, he came to me. We didn't know if we could get a station wagon through the snow, so we got out the jeep and fixed a sled behind." Only then did Jenny peer through the window at the odd-looking thing waiting outside her door.

"Then what are we waiting for?" She was on her feet, ready to go. Jeff smiled at the upturned face.

"Not a thing." They hurried out to the jeep and drove off into the darkness.

Chapter 10

If I live to be a hundred I'll never forget this night, Jenny thought numbly. The threatening sky of the afternoon had blossomed into a full-scale mountain storm. Sleet, sharp stinging snow, hard and relentless, poured down on Jeff and her as they fought their way across the valley to where Lance lay helpless in the tiny cabin. A thousand thoughts rushed through the girl's brain. Had Dr. Scofield and Ann reached the cabin safely? And if so, what had they found? Was Lance all right? Prayers, mingled now and then with a sob she valiantly tried to hold back, alternated with mental images of what they might find. Don, huddled in the back, was totally silent.

"Please, dear God, let him be all right." Jenny hadn't realized she had spoken aloud until Jeff answered.

"Don't torture yourself, Jenny. God isn't going to let a man like Lance die. There's too much left for him to do in this world. I thought it over all the way to your place, and I honestly don't think it will be permitted."

Jenny started in surprise. His words had been such a reflection of her own thoughts. Patting the firm arm occupied in maneuvering the jeep along the increasingly difficult road, she felt a little of the peace and strength that characterized Jeff steal into her own being. Falling silent, she peered ahead into the murky darkness, willing the snow to stop, willing the brave little jeep to make it.

If I live to be a hundred I'll never forget this night, Dr. Scofield thought anxiously. It had taken Ann and him some time to return to the cabin, and when they reached it, Lance still hadn't regained consciousness. Only his deep, quiet breathing told them he was still alive. Now there was time for a more thorough examination. The deft, supple fingers of the man who had gained a high surgeon's post probed, felt, discovered, until with a sigh he stood to his feet, meeting Ann's eyes squarely.

"He's going to be all right. There is no sign of internal injuries. There is a whopping big knot on his back where he fell, but it will only leave a large bruised area. It wasn't over the kidneys, so we don't have to worry about that. None of the major organs seem to be affected."

"But why hasn't he regained consciousness?"

Dr. Scofield chuckled a bit, relieving the tension in the fear-filled room. Parting Lance's hair, he showed Ann a large bump on the back of the head. Evidently Lance had not only struck the outcropping log with his back but had also banged his head when he went down. "When he wakes up, he's going to have the granddaddy of all headaches!"

Ann's white face relaxed in a smile. If Dr. Scofield could laugh, things must be all right. Turning away, she stared out the window. "I hope they get here soon. It's really bad out there."

Dr. Scofield looked over her shoulder, a tiny frown crossing his face. He didn't tell her how bad it *really* was. He had taken quick stock of the cabin. The tenderfoot must have gone for supplies. There was very little on hand and nothing to feed an injured man. If the storm continued, all three of them could be in real trouble. Wisely he kept it to himself. Time enough later to make Ann aware of their danger. Besides, Jeff or Jingles or Don would get through if any human could face that storm.

Many miles away, Twilight paced the floor, holding Tommy Two close. If I live to be a hundred I won't forget this night, she vowed silently. It had taken all her strength to watch Jeff prepare to challenge the storm ahead, yet not for anything would she have held him back. It was Lance out there, her sister's husband. She thought of the way he had taken such wonderful care of her when little Tommy was born, of the dozens of ways he had carved a little spot in the hearts of the Stehekin people with his tireless and loving care of them all.

Quick tears sprang to her eyes as she thought of the look in his face at the wedding just a few nights before. She didn't understand just what it was that kept Lance and Jenny from happiness, but there was something there. Obviously Lance loved Jenny hopelessly. It was equally apparent Jenny was head over heels in love with her husband. But yet there was that something . . . Twilight shook her head impatiently.

Bowing her head, she prayed in the same childlike, trusting way her sister had done. The sound of her words caused the child in her arms to open his eyes and look up at her in wonderment. "Please take care of

Lance. We all need him so much, especially Jenny. Please . . ."

Comforted, she turned away. It was time for Tommy Two to be put down. She must not stand there dawdling any longer. In the busyness of caring for the baby, she lost track of time until someone knocked at the door. It was Aunt Lucy and Jingles, tired and drooping on the porch.

"We didn't think we could make it even this far," Aunt Lucy told her. "The storm is getting worse every minute."

They slumped into chairs by the fire, welcoming the heat that set their wet clothing steaming. Twilight saw the strained look in Aunt Lucy's face, but Jingles as usual had the last word.

"If you're worrying about all of them, don't. They'll be all right. It was earlier when they went. The storm wasn't so bad."

Twilight was glad they had brought it out in the open. Just their presence had calmed her greatly. "If the storm continues, they'll be short of food. Surely there wouldn't be much in the cabin!"

Aunt Lucy reassured her this time. "Don't worry about that. There's not a storm so bad Jingles can't eventually get through!"

Color came back into Twilight's face. For a moment, her worry had blotted out knowledge of Jingles. She knew Aunt Lucy's words were true. So many times Jingles had gone into the worst mountain storms, bringing back those who were lost even when the most adverse and perverse conditions reigned. In a day or so, he could get to the stranded little group.

"Besides, with all the medical help there," Aunt Lucy said, "we don't have that to worry over."

Twilight laughed outright this time, counting on her fingers. "Lance, Dr. Scofield, Jenny, Ann."

"To say nothing of Don," Jingles put in. "Don't leave him out of the lineup. He's quite a resourceful guy."'

Twilight laughed again. It was true. If the little group in the cabin had been handpicked, they couldn't have been more perfectly selected.

But in the little cabin surrounded by a howling blizzard, there was no laughter. Lance had finally come around, puzzled and amazed. He even sat up, propped against the decrepit bedstead, with Dr. Scofield and Ann watching anxiously. The blazing fire provided warmth, but the thoughts of the three were far away and serious. Lance wasn't out of danger yet. A fall like that could leave problems. . . .

The hours wore away, tick by tick, minute by minute. Each of the three imprisoned in the rude shelter made a pretense of not looking at his watch, vainly trying to hide from the others his growing anxiety. Ann and Dr. Scofield could feel the rising concern and frustration in Lance because he lay there helpless, while help was probably out in the storm, on its way even at that moment. It was bad enough in the cabin. What must it be like outside?

Yet when Jeff, Jenny, and Don burst into the room, the waiting three were so dazed, it took them a minute to realize the others had actually come!

Dr. Scofield came forward with arms out, but Ann brushed by him. Like a homing bird to its nest of little ones, she flew straight to Don, who told her, "He heard us, Ann. He heard us!"

"Who heard you?"

"God." A curious stillness settled over the group at his reply. "Jenny asked Him to help and He did."

For a moment the only sound was Dr. Scofield blowing his nose, hard. Jenny had hesitated in the doorway, eyes enormous, wondering what her welcome would be. But her first glance at Lance dispelled all the bright hopes she had built up on the way to him. Perhaps he would forgive her, accept her . . . but no, his eyes wore the same cool look they had held before.

If she could have known how his heart was pounding, she might have taken hope, but he only said, "Nice of you to drop in, Jenny . . . and to pray."

Jenny's brave front faltered. "I asked God, but the storm was terrible, and . . ." Her voice trailed off.

Dr. Scofield came to the rescue in his own way. "Well, He made that storm, so He can just make a way through it!"

This time there was laughter. They had so much to be thankful for, it was best not to look back and dwell on what had happened. If only the storm would cease, they would have no trouble, and yet as Dr. Scofield said, didn't they expect to receive help when they asked for it? This was the thought in all of their minds.

The storm didn't let up that night, or all the next day. Sometimes Jenny thought they would be buried alive with the snow. If it hadn't been for the food shortage, she would have enjoyed the confinement, she thought guiltily, seeing the set look on the others' faces. Twilight would surely be frantic by now.

The morning of the third day dawned on the weary group. A stray beam of sunlight shone through the uncurtained window of the shack, gently revealing to them that the storm was over.

"Thank God!" Lance's heartfelt whisper echoed each of their own thoughts.

They had eaten the last of the small stores the night before. Evidently the tenderfoot had let his supplies get very low before deciding to stock up. He had very little left that was edible. Lance's back and head kept him miserable. Dr. Scofield wanted to get him to a place where he could be treated, as quickly as possible.

The welcome sunlight promised all kinds of good things. Relief from the gray outlook, the lack of food. Rescue. That was the big word in each heart. But as the day grew on and once again great masses of clouds began to cover the shivering sky, the hope generated in the morning began to fail. No one spoke of it, but many times they turned their heads, refusing to meet each other's eyes. If another storm came . . .

It was late afternoon before they faced the reality of having to stay longer in their snowbound shelter. Jeff and Don had quietly stocked the hut with as much wood as they could drag in. Jenny and Ann had melted snow and boiled it. There was no stream close enough to get to through the great drifts of snow. At least they would have warmth and water. Then they settled again to wait.

It was just about dark when a loud shout attracted their attention. If an angel from heaven had appeared at that moment, it wouldn't have been any more welcome than Jingles. He had borrowed the largest snow cat in the community and, spending all day breaking a trail, had made it through.

"Don't waste time in rejoicing," he commanded tersely, watching the lowering sky. "We've got to get out of here, and fast!"

It didn't take long to bundle them into the different conveyances. Jingles went ahead with the large snow cat. Don and Ann took the smaller one, which Dr. Scofield dramatically refused to touch again.

He rode with Lance on the sled, over Jenny's protests, while she was put in with Jeff, who drove the jeep pulling the sled as carefully as though he were hauling a load of fresh-laid eggs.

It was a long time before they reached Jingles's ranch, to find Aunt Lucy and Twilight in the doorway. Jingles and Aunt Lucy had stayed with Twilight the first night of the adventure, and had taken her and Tommy Two home with them the next morning. Now Jingles swung into the yard with a grand gesture.

"All safe and sound!" His reassuring words reached Aunt Lucy and Twilight only seconds before the two women came over to him and Jeff, tears and laughter mingling.

By the time they were all inside the capacious farmhouse, the sky was again filled with swirling, menacing flakes. Was it possible that nature now took revenge for being cheated of her victims? Whatever the cause, the storm raged even more furiously than it had before. Only now it didn't matter. All were safe inside, warm. Lance was put to bed, Jenny hovering over him until Dr. Scofield told her she was spoiling her husband rotten. The shadow of fear still lurked in the depths of her big brown eyes, but it was gradually subsiding.

"What happened to the shivaree?" Ann wanted to know. She was greeted with hoots and catcalls. Shivarees were supposed to be surprises.

177

"My beautiful prune pies," Jenny mourned, in mock sorrow.

Aunt Lucy was practical. "The longer they sit, the better they are." She was so thrilled to have them all there, she couldn't hold it back any longer. "Do any of you know what day it is?"

They looked at her in confusion.

Ann counted on her fingers. "Let's see. We were married." She blushed and looked at Don, "Then there were three days of storm, and some days in between . . ."

Honey and Tommy, who had been round-eyed at the story of rescue, couldn't keep still any longer. "It's Christmas Eve!"

The grownups, with the exception of Aunt Lucy, gaped. It was Christmas Eve, a snowy, stormy Christmas Eve.

"Can we hang up our stockings?" Honey wanted to know.

Aunt Lucy opened her mouth to speak, but Tommy was ahead of her. "You can't put in any stocking the presents we got this Christmas." He pointed to the group around the fire. "God brought all of them back." His meaning was clear. For a moment, all of them were once again brought back to the reality of the terrible storm, the anxiety, the waiting.

Aunt Lucy put her arm around Honey.

"You go right ahead and hang up your stocking, Honey, and you, too." She looked at Tommy. "I wouldn't be a bit surprised if . . ." Her tone was deliberately mysterious, and Honey's face brightened. She was still enough of a child to want all the little extras that go with Christmas.

"We'll have a double Christmas," Ann promised. "Aunt Lucy has invited us all to stay for a few days for a Christmas party, and as soon as the snow is lighter, maybe even tomorrow, we can go home and get our gifts for one another."

But as they went to bed that night each of them remembered Tommy's words. "God brought all of them back." It was the best Christmas Eve any of them had ever known.

True to Ann's predictions, the world again grew brilliantly light with sunshine the next morning. Jingles, Don, and Jeff were able to go to Jeff's place, to Don's, and last of all to the "honeymoon cottage" and pick up all the carefully wrapped packages, as well as some surprises of their own.

What a Christmas! Aunt Lucy had a way with a turkey and dressing that no one else could duplicate. Jenny's prune pies seemed to have improved with age. Twilight contributed her own skill in preparing various vegetables, and Ann whipped up a batch each of fudge and divinity. But the highlight of the day came that evening.

The gifts had been exchanged. The dinner was only a memory, while the candy dishes remained half filled. The lights had been turned low; competition with the fire and softly glowing candles on the mantel was nonexistent. It was time for giving thanks.

Jingles's voice was rich and deep as he sang, "Oh, holy night . . ."

Jeff's voice was unsteady as he read the beautiful story of the child born in a manger on the first Christmas, from the second chapter of the gospel of Luke. Even the younger ones were held by its ever-new, yet familiar words. Jenny sat by Lance, where he lay on the couch. Ann and Don were absorbed in the story. Twilight and the baby gave reality to the tale they listened to, as meaningful in their own lives as it had been so long ago.

How joyous were their carols that Christmas Eve! The shadow of what could have been tragedy was exorcised by the beautiful old songs. Everything from "Jingle Bells" to the last and most fitting, "Silent Night," was sung. Old voices.

Young voices. Voices of praise. Voices of love and appreciation.

"If I live to be a hundred, I will never forget this night," Aunt Lucy exclaimed.

The words were familiar, but it was for Ann, the irrepressible, to add the final comment. "That's what I thought a couple of nights ago — but for quite different reasons!"

The spell was broken. There was leftover pie and turkey and all the snacks that are so appreciated following Christmas dinner. Much later, when the children had gone to bed, Ann and Don had drifted to their room, and Twilight and Jeff were busily putting Tommy Two down for the night, only Jingles, Aunt Lucy, Lance, and Jenny were still before the fireplace. They hated to see the evening end.

"How would you like to see something you've probably never seen before?" Jingles asked them, nonchalantly waving a piece of paper in his hand.

Aunt Lucy looked up suspiciously. "What are you up to?"

He smiled mysteriously. Counting on his fingers, he told them, "Jeff and Twilight have seen it, and besides, Tommy Two's too young to travel much. Don has seen it, but Ann hasn't, so that makes two. Jenny and Lance haven't, so that's two more. We've seen it but would like to again, so would Honey and Tommy. That's eight. I have here in my hand" — he paused for dramatic effect — "eight reservations at Leavenworth."

"Leavenworth? Oh, the Bavarian village!" Jenny's eyes danced. Lance recalled going through it on his way over from Seattle the summer before.

"It will be beautiful," Jingles told them. "Even though the actual lighting of the Christmas lights celebration was the first Saturday in December, all the lights will still be up. Lance, can you make it in another week?"

With all his heart Lance wanted to shout yes, but caution held him back. Naturally a motel reservation would have been made for him and Jenny. No separate bedrooms there. If only she cared, how different it could have been! They were all waiting for his answer, he had to say something.

Throwing caution to the winds, he spoke recklessly. "You bet! I've been wanting to take Jenny for a long time. That little town pulled itself out of a slump and worked together to make a tourist haven. I noticed it when I came through. Just one thing." His tone was casual. "With this back I may not be too easy to put up with. Get Jenny and me two rooms, so my thrashing around won't bother her." No one noticed Jenny's sigh of relief. She hadn't known how to get around her predicament without flatly refusing to go.

When the others had gone to their rooms, she lingered by the couch for a few moments before going upstairs.

"Thank you, Lance." He never knew how close to tears she was at that moment.

He could only feel his own pain, and it showed through his reply. "Sure, Guinevere. Anything to please the lady."

She turned away, and once again any hope of reconciliation had passed, leaving them both more desolate than they had ever been before.

Chapter 11

Never had Jenny seen anything more beautiful than Leavenworth at Christmastime. She couldn't pick out one thing more than another that made it so lovely. First, the setting itself was one of outdoor grandeur. The little town was set in the heart of frosted hills, snow touching their tops like a benediction. It was composed largely of one main street, with other streets spraying off. There was a small park in the center, sporting an old-fashioned bandstand for summer concerts. It bore the German welcome sign, *"Wilkommen zu Leavenworth,"* with the jolly figure of an Alpine climber.

And the shops themselves!

"I could spend a week in just one of them," she confided to Ann.

Her friend smiled in sympathy with Jenny's excitement. She felt the same way! Each of the shops had been remodeled in Bavarian style. The words *"edelweiss"* and "Tyrol" were everywhere, along with lesser-known but equally descriptive terms. Highlighting the entire street were the strings and strings of Christmas lights.

The homes were festive in their brightness, each outdoing the next with its decorations. It seemed trite to say it was indeed a fairyland, but Jenny could think of no other word.

Then there were the people.

"Have you ever felt more at home in a strange town?" It was Lance who posed that question. The whole town seemed so glad to welcome them there. Despite the fact that thousands of tourists each year gathered for their festivals, Lance felt that he himself had been welcomed with joy simply because he came!

"Told you you'd like it." Jingles's eyes twinkled. "Listen!"

Standing on the corner, they heard the deep-toned carillon bells start their hourly pealing. They had learned that day that the people of Leavenworth had had a record made of the carillon bells and sold thousands of dollars worth of the records to pay for the beautiful chiming bells. Each of the three families had bought a record, and now that same carillon chiming throughout the town caught at their throats with its sheer loveliness.

"Joy to the world, the Lord is come!" rang the bells. Joy, gladness, hope — the world of misery and sickness seemed far away at that moment. Close to Lance's side, Jenny was so moved, it seemed almost more than she could bear. Even the stars seemed to shine benevolently on them. And yet there was more to come — if only things were at peace between her and Lance!

"Time to eat." Jingles's pronouncement was hailed with delight. They hadn't realized how hungry the crisp air had made them. With the familiarity of frequent visits to the area, Jingles led them to one of the Bavarian restaurants, although as he explained in a rumbling undertone, "They're all excellent. This one is indicative of the service and food you'd get anywhere in town."

They were ushered into a long room with chandeliers, a beautiful fireplace, and carefully set tables. The Christmas motif blended with the Bavarian touch set the tone for pure fun and gaiety. And the food! From cheese fondue through a huge meal to apple strudel, they groaned, protesting they couldn't eat one more bite — that is, until the next course was served!

"I'd gain ten pounds if I stayed here very long," Jenny told Lance.

His answer was typical. "Then we'll take

you home now. No butterball for me, please."

The last words were picked up by the jaunty waitress who smiled all the time, eager to please. "No butter, sir?"

He laughed, then relaxed back as the entertainment came on. It was superb! Yodelers, accordionists, harmony beyond description. The whole town seemed filled with the music of Christmas.

Honey and Tommy were round-eyed at the clever costumes of the entertainers, and when Honey shyly asked, "Do you know Jingle Bells?" it was sung directly to her!

"What a fun place," Jenny whispered, uncomfortably aware of the closeness the little table had required.

Lance, with a look around to see no one was listening, told her, "Nice place for a honeymoon."

In an instant, all her joy was gone, a stricken look replacing the happiness of a moment before.

It was too much for Lance. "I'm sorry, Jenny. Let's try to be friends, at least."

She could only nod, and for a bare moment his hand touched hers. To hide her emotion, she pulled away and pretended to search in her wallet. The others hadn't noticed. They were still enthralled with the place.

"I want to come back again," Ann stated firmly. Her sidelong glance at Don spoke volumes. It was still part of their honeymoon, and they didn't care who knew it. Jingles noticed the look and beamed. Nothing like folks being in love to brighten up a vacation, he told himself.

"Well," he drawled, eyes bright, teasing Aunt Lucy. "There's plenty of reason to come back. In addition to the Christmas lights celebration, there's the winter snowmobile races, the ski jumping, the May festival, the —"

Aunt Lucy interrupted. "But my favorite is the Washington State Autumn Leaf Festival."

"Autumn Leaf Festival? What's that?" several voices asked.

"Nine days of special events, music, theater, dancing, in celebration of the arrival of the fall colors. It's the last weekend in September through the first weekend in October, and if anything is beautiful, that is."

"It couldn't be more beautiful than now," Jenny said.

Aunt Lucy shook her head. "I can't compare. You don't compare apples and oranges, do you? These are as different as apples and oranges, but mark my words, you'll fall in love with Leavenworth in the autumn time."

Jingles took up the cudgels in her defense. "That's right," he said. "Place looks like it's on fire. Red, orange, yellow, gold, bronze — you can't put your camera down."

"But we might not be here in the fall," Jenny mourned. "We might be in Seattle."

"So what? It's only a two or two-and-a-half-hour drive over. Lance surely can drive that far on a weekend, even if he's had a rough week!"

Lance vowed to do exactly that because he was intoxicated with the place and because it would please Jenny. It was a small thing. But it might help to win back her love.

At last it was time to go. Stuffed, happy, the group made their way back to their motel. Even it was Bavarian style, and very quiet.

"I've never seen the Big Dipper so low in the sky," Jenny commented as they walked out of the station wagon.

"Lack of air pollution." As usual, Jingles's terse explanation wasted no words, but was perfectly clear in meaning. It was true. The air was clean, pure, but oh, so cold! How cold and shiny even the stars seemed — and how large.

"Wonder just what the temperature is?" Jenny walked over to an outdoor thermometer. "Five below zero?" She was amazed. It didn't feel quite *that* cold!

"Dry cold, you don't feel it so much," Jingles said.

But she was glad for the warm blankets provided by the motel, especially the next morning. She awakened early. There was no sound from the adjoining bedroom. Lance must still be asleep. She had heard him moving restlessly in the night and longed to go care for him. But she hesitated, heart pounding, and soon she heard no more. He must have fallen asleep again. Asleep again . . . Jenny couldn't keep her eyes open.

The next time she awakened, Lance was up, calling her. She could smell his shaving lotion when she headed for the bathroom.

He was all ready. "What a sleepyhead!" His tone was light, almost teasing.

Jenny couldn't believe her ears. She had no way of knowing that during those restless moments the night before, Lance had decided the only course open to him was to fight by apparent nonresistance. If Jenny could only accept him as a friend, then a friend is what he would be. He still didn't want a wife, even Jenny, without all her love, or simply because she bore his name and perhaps felt obligated to him.

Their day was once again spent enjoying the friendly and warm atmosphere mingled with the spicy, cold air of Leavenworth. Just for fun, Don and Ann went into a real estate office, only to come out with a stunned look on their faces.

"I can't believe it," Ann sputtered. "Those prices for real estate are outrageous!"

"You aren't the only one who thinks Leavenworth is pretty special," Aunt Lucy reminded. "A lot of folks who don't want the isolation of a place like Stehekin, but who want freedom from cities, are discovering this place. I doubt that there are more than three or four places in town or the surrounding area you could buy at any price! This little town is almost perfect. In addition to the friendly people and beautiful location, there's a completely equipped hospital. Then, too, Wenatchee is just a little farther on, in case of a major medical problem."

When they finally drove away that evening each looked back with different feelings.

"I'd like to always remember it this way," Jenny said softly, once more devouring the scene with her eyes, storing up the Christmas magic.

The others didn't put their feelings in words until Tommy added, "I liked the food, it was swell!" He looked surprised when they all laughed. Filling him had been like filling a silo, only he didn't stay full as long. He had eaten three of the biggest hotcakes known to mankind that morning, along with ham, eggs, and hash browns, yet in a few hours had been clamoring for lunch!

Honey was tired and sleepy, clutching a dried-apple doll that had been dressed in scraps of bright blue cotton imprinted with tiny flowers and complete with frilly, Bavarian-style apron. The big station wagon purred along, and although the roads were starting to get a little icy, there was no snow.

They had gone about a mile from town when it happened, bringing a tragic end to their perfect vacation. As they were slowing for a curve, the car behind them pulled out in a bad spot to try to pass.

"Crazy darn fool!" Jingles tried to get out of his way, but the little sports car hit an icy patch and spun directly into their path.

"Look out!" Lance clutched Jenny with a grip of iron, and the others braced themselves. Then came the crash. The heavy station wagon staggered under the impact, but under Jingles's expert guidance it managed to stop short of the road's edge. The sports car wasn't so fortunate. After hitting the wagon, it bounced back against the guard rail and across the road into a large evergreen tree, coming up against the sturdy trunk with a resounding bang.

"Is anyone in here hurt?" The doctor in Lance took immediate command, even as he was opening the door to go to the aid of the driver of the other car.

"Just shook up," was Jingles's response.

The others nodded. They had been protected by the heaviness of their wagon.

Lance jerked open the door of the sports car. Only one person in it, thank God. The passenger's side was completely caved in.

"Are you hurt? I'm a doctor," he told the dazed youth.

The boy shook his head. "I'm all right." Gingerly he stepped from the car, but as he took a step forward, he collapsed into Lance's arms, his right leg bent at a bad angle.

By the time Lance had him lowered to the ground, Jenny and Ann were there with blankets from the wagon.

"Is it bad?" Ann asked.

"Fractured right leg, plus this." Lance was busily engaged in stanching the flow of blood from a cut in the boy's head. "You'll be all right," he assured the boy. The scream of an ambulance cut short his sentence. Evidently the farmer who lived at the scene of the accident had seen it happen and phoned back to Leavenworth.

"I'll go with him," Lance decided, still holding the gaping edges of the head wound together. It wasn't deep, but it was long, and the bleeding was profuse. Applying steady pressure, Lance climbed into the ambulance with the boy, leaving the others to follow. As soon as they arrived at the hospital, Jenny and Ann introduced themselves as nurses, wondering if they could be of assistance.

"You're a godsend," the weary head nurse told them. "We've had a rash of accidents tonight, and we're shorthanded. Seems cold and flu season has hit our staff. If you could help out, we'd really appreciate it."

There was no question about it. Leaving the girls and Lance, Aunt Lucy and Jingles took Don and the kids back to their motel. It wouldn't hurt anything for them to stay another day.

"Can I be a nurse when I grow up?" Honey wanted to know. "So I can help people?"

"And can I be a doctor?" Tommy put in. "Then I could come back to Stehekin when Dr. Scofield and Lance retire." There was enough seriousness in their tone that Jingles and Aunt Lucy didn't laugh.

Don, the quiet one, told them, "You can be anything you want to be if you work hard."

It seemed to satisfy them, and it was without protest that they even went to bed early.

"I'll bet you're pretty proud of that gal of yours," Jingles told Don warmly. "Not too many young women who'd give up a day of their honeymoon to help out a short-handed hospital staff."

"She wouldn't be Ann if she didn't," Don said softly. He couldn't voice the full pride he felt in Ann, and the continual wonder that a beautiful girl like her, beautiful both inside and outside, could have ever fallen for a plain, country guy like himself. He forgot the outstanding record he was making as a ranger, as well as his many fine qualities.

Not so Ann. Just then she and Jenny

were getting ready to help Lance set the boy's bone.

"Don's the most understanding guy on earth," she said solemnly. "How many men would let their brand-new wife out of sight for even one day of their honeymoon?"

Jenny nodded, her eyes bright. She knew exactly how Ann felt. But there was no time for further confidences. Lance was waiting for them — or, as she later told Ann, Dr. Reeves was waiting for them. When he put on his surgical gown and mask, he was no longer just her own Lance, but the doctor who belonged heart and soul to whatever patient he was serving. His commands were crisp and sure. There was no nonsense about him, and Jenny was only a helper, nothing more, in that room of healing.

The bone-setting went beautifully, but before they finished, another case was brought in needing attention. The other doctors who weren't on sick leave were busy, so Lance and the girls were asked to help with that one, and another, and another.

"Whew!" Ann mopped her face wearily as, finally, in between patients, she and Jenny joined Lance for a steaming bowl of hot soup. Only then did they realize that the night was nearly over and they were hungry. Never had they been busier, even back in the Seattle hospital. But how worthwhile was the feeling that crept from toes to heart to head, that they had used their skill to help others in need.

Later that morning they stood at the window looking out on a clear, bright winter day. The crisis was over. All the patients were doing nicely, and several of the staff had called in that they were improved and would be back the next day. Could they stay one more night? the supervisor wanted to know.

"Certainly." Lance spoke for all three. "Just give us a few hours of rest, and we'll come back at four this afternoon."

The girls nodded. They were needed here. There was no question about their staying. They also had fullest confidence in Jingles, Aunt Lucy, and Don to know they would approve.

That night was another experience to remember. Although much quieter than the evening before, it was like stepping back into a familiar but long-ago world. After the days at Stehekin, the routine of night duty on the wards was quite a contrast! Small flashlights in hand, the girls silently stole from bed to bed, checking charts and patients without disturbing them, except when necessary to administer medication.

"It's really a different world," Ann whispered once in passing. "All the Christmas gaiety outside, people in trouble, sick, hurt, in here. I'm glad they have such a nice hospital."

Jenny agreed.

Later, she bumped into Lance, who was also having a quiet night.

"Jenny." He took advantage of the empty hall to cup her small hands between his two strong ones. "Jenny . . . friends?"

"Friends, Lance." There was so much more that could be said, but the words trembled unspoken within each of them. And yet the moment was one to be buried deep into each heart, to lie there glowing. It was a moment of sharing, togetherness.

Why, Jenny thought, as she watched the tall figure stride down the hall to care for another patient, this is what marriage is all about. This is how it could be, if only . . . As so many times before, she pushed away those two little words, "if only." Surely Lance would forgive and love her in time . . . or would he? Well, whether or not he ever did, at least she had caught a glimpse of what real marriage could be. It was like a great truth shining through the fog of day-to-day living. True marriage wasn't merely based on physical closeness. True marriage was also the spiritual sharing of man and woman.

A great pity swept over the tired nurse as she thought of those "modern" people who chased rainbows of elusive happiness, looking for a new marriage partner, over and over again, trying to find fulfillment. They will never find it, she knew suddenly. I would rather be in this awkward position, married and yet not a wife, than to be in their places. Sometime, somehow, he will care, she determined. Then I can tell him it was always Lancelot who held first place in my heart. Someday . . .

Did Lance feel as Jenny had felt in that moment of so many unspoken words? Yes, a rush of gladness had swept over him. At least she didn't hate him. The resentment inside, which had grown ever since she had told him she loved another man, receded. When she looked up at him with those clear, trusting eyes, it had been almost more than he could stand not to proclaim his love then and there. But the hospital was no place for it. Besides, he had made a promise to himself. This time he would keep it. They would go back to being friends, partners, people who trusted one another.

And the other man? Pooh! Lance dismissed him with a flick of his fingers. Whoever it was was far away. A small smile warmed his features, causing his patients to wonder why this tired doctor could so casually smile at this time of night. But not one of them understood it was because he was looking forward to a time in the future . . . Someday . . .

Chapter 12

Incredible as it seemed, the Seattle hospital accepted Dr. Scofield's outlandish proposition. They wanted to keep him at any cost, even if it only meant part of the year. Then, too, they knew and appreciated Dr. Reeves. If Dr. Scofield felt he could head up the surgery unit, then there was no question. Dr. Reeves was their man. He was to start as soon as he and Jenny could move from Stehekin.

"Do you really want to go?" Twilight asked Jenny curiously, as they were carefully packing dishes and utensils. Jenny's busy hands stilled. She wanted to be totally honest, not only with Twilight, but with herself.

"Yes, I do." She surprised herself and Twilight. "Not only will it mean a wonderful opportunity for Lance, but it will give me a greater variety of opportunities to use my nursing skills. Twilight, there is so much I don't know! The more I learn, the more there is to learn. This will put me back in touch with new methods and let me practice some of the things I am not able to get here in Stehekin. You know I didn't get much ward duty after graduation!"

Twilight's laughter joined her own. There was a softness since the Leavenworth trip. Twilight couldn't help but wonder if Jenny and Lance hadn't resolved at least part of their problem. Yet she knew whatever it was had not been completely taken care of. When Jenny didn't know her sister was watching, there was a tired droop to her mouth. Perhaps these months in Seattle would be good for her.

"Don't forget to come back."

"We won't. Lance says they want him to stay until the first of May this year because of the late start. From now on, it will be from October first to April first in Seattle, and then" — she flung her arms wide — "summer in Stehekin."

"I'm glad you're going to go back, Jenny." The words sounded strange coming from Twilight, and Jenny stared in surprise, a little hurt.

"Don't get me wrong. We love having you here, but Lance has a gift that shouldn't be limited to only a small community. There is work for you both that needs to be shared. When you have talents such as you both possess, they must be used for all people, not selfishly."

Jenny only nodded. It was the same thing she felt.

There was a little group gathered to see them off the next day. Jeff and Twilight, with Tommy Two carefully wrapped against the winter day. Don and Ann, as happy in their own love as Jeff and Twilight. Tommy and Honey. And, of course, Aunt Lucy and Jingles.

"Don't forget to come home, you two," Jingles said.

Quick tears filled Jenny's eyes. She felt torn in two as the mail boat slipped away from the landing, leaving the figures on shore to grow smaller and smaller before being lost altogether in the growing mist. Yet how could she be sad with so much excitement ahead of her?

Lance divined her thoughts. "Know what, Guinevere?" The deep timbre in his voice that was reserved for special moments set her heart tingling. "When we get to Seattle, as much as time permits, we're going to do all the things we should have done before we were married!"

"Such as?" she asked.

His smile was jaunty. "You're going to

get courted, Guinevere. Courted. Kind of an old-fashioned word, isn't it? But then, you're a little old-fashioned yourself."

Flags of mock indignation waved their bright banners in her face as she retorted, "Old-fashioned? How about you, Lancelot? You were as excited over that shivaree that finally took place for Don and Ann as I was, and if there ever was an old-fashioned custom, that was it!"

Lance laughed outright. It *had* been fun. Though it was long delayed, or perhaps because it had been, Ann and Don had been completely taken by surprise. When their friends and neighbors arrived about eleven one Friday night, banging pans, tooting horns, demanding they get up and have a party, they were amazed. Ann thought it had been forgotten in the excitement of the blizzard. Rosy, laughing, she had donned a long robe, welcomed them all in, and they spent a merry evening according to local tradition, ending with all the goodies the different women had brought. And yes, Jenny's prune pies were again present!

"You're really a pretty good cook," Lance told her cockily. "Don't you get me fat with all your baking."

"I won't have as much time when I'm

working full-time."

Jenny's words were prophetic. Once she and Lance had settled comfortably in the large, airy second-floor apartment at the Matthewsons', there was scarcely a minute she was free. In a frenzy of domesticity, she remade drapes, curtains, and slip covers, but that was only in the first week. After that, she had all she could do to work, take care of the charming little home, and still be free to be courted, as Lance had so quaintly put it.

Had there ever been a man like Lance? The question forced its way into her consciousness daily. True to his word, her husband took advantage of every spare moment to be with her doing something special. They explored Seattle, from Queen Anne Hill to the underground city, from the government locks to the beautiful University of Washington campus, from the Space Needle and Monorail to the quiet beauty of the many parks. They went to them all. Sometimes there was a little time for one of the excellent restaurants in the area. One weekend, they went to Mt. Rainier, with its glistening white top raised against the sky.

And yet through it all, Lance treated her as a special guest, nothing more, nothing less. They had settled into the two-bedroom apartment as naturally as they had done at Stehekin. There was no sentiment evident. Still, at times Jenny could see a curious glint in Lance's eyes. He had never been a patient man. Now he had forced himself to a role unnatural, believing it the best.

One evening that would always stand out in Jenny's memory was Valentine's night. There was a banquet for the hospital staff at one of the larger restaurants. The women were asked to come in the pinks, reds, and whites associated with the holiday.

"Wear your wedding dress, Jenny," Lance had suggested. "There just isn't another dress you could buy that would be so suited for you." He grinned. "Besides, very few of our colleagues have seen it anyway, now that Ann is in Stehekin."

She couldn't resist him when he looked like that. So when they appeared that night, she was gowned in white lace, a huge corsage of red carnations pinned to her shoulder. Lance had bought the flowers on his way home. Even though there was barely time left for him to shower and change, he wanted Jenny to have the flowers. When he saw her glowing, clear brown eyes and the way her face reflected the rosiness of his offering, he was especially glad to have taken the time.

She was beautiful — and she was his! Satisfaction oozed from him as they entered the large room set aside for the banquet. His friendship pact seemed to be paying off. In time . . .

The hall had been decorated for the event. Red and white streamers presented a false ceiling, great masses of carnations similar to Jenny's banked the wall behind the speaker's stand and graced the individual tables. To their surprise, Lance and Jenny were led to the head table. When dinner was over, the reason came out. The chief of staff rose. Various awards were presented. Then the chief turned and motioned to Lance.

"We have no special paper or engraved award tonight for one of our number. But I do want to give special attention and recognition to this man. He has fought against what must at times have seemed hopeless. He has won the admiration of every person on the staff. For this valiant battle, I wish to personally commend Dr. Lance Reeves and his charming wife, Jennet." A storm of applause drowned the speaker out for a moment, but he motioned for silence.

"This fight is what prompted us to consider the odd proposal Dr. Scofield made regarding a split-shift between here and Stehekin. Probably no other doctors on the staff would have been granted this privilege. But with Dr. Scofield summers, and Dr. Reeves winters, we can't go far wrong!" This time there was no denying the crowd. With one accord they were on their feet, seconding by their enthusiasm what the chief had said.

Lance and Jenny sat amazed. It was too much. Cries of "Speech, speech" were coming from the cheering group. Even in her pride, Jenny noticed there was no jealousy on the faces of those other doctors and nurses. This in itself was a tribute to the way they felt about Lance. There were only good wishes and appreciation for the job he was doing. A little shiver went up her spine. What if she hadn't been willing to leave Stehekin so he could serve here? Thank heaven they had left. It had been right for them to come back, she knew that.

Lance was on his feet, speechless. What could he say? He had never expected such tribute. He was saved by the paging system of the restaurant.

"Paging Dr. Simpson. Paging Dr. Reeves. Paging Dr. Jones." The mechanical voice went on and on, naming various doctors. Those were the ones on call tonight, Jenny realized, listening intently. A hush fell over the room. "Report to your hospital immediately, please."

Before any of them could move, a white-faced waitress entered. "There has been an explosion in one of the factories downtown. They are bringing a lot of injured people in. They asked all of you who can get to the hospital immediately to do so. It's an emergency."

The banquet hall was a confusion of doctors and nurses rushing to go on duty, while their spouses or dates made arrangements to drop each other off. Jenny went with Lance, hurrying out to their car. She would be needed as much as he would this night.

The emergency room was almost chaos. Patients came in a steady stream. Some of the injured had been taken to other hospitals in the city, but since theirs was the closest to the factory, Lance and Jenny's hospital received the most. It was a night of horror. Ambulances screaming, police sirens preceding them, cutting through the city traffic. Burned human beings, some almost beyond recognition. Gone was the happy spirit of Valentine's Day. It was indeed an emergency. Worse. It was a nightmare. Jenny lost track of how many first-aid-type injuries she cared for, releasing one patient after another as rapidly as she could. She also moved from stretcher to stretcher, making sure that doctors tended to the most serious cases as quickly as possible.

The relatives were almost as much of a problem as the injured. They stormed the doors, wanting to know if loved ones were all right. At last, in sheer desperation, the hospital had two policemen ushering the frantic people into another area until word could be brought to them of the condition of the patients.

"You're hindering the doctors. Please move outside," one policeman told a persistent, sobbing woman. "I know it's your husband, but these people can't take care of him unless you leave them alone." Ironically, it turned out that the woman's husband had gotten off easily — a deep burn on the left hand, painful but not serious. In a little while, he was leading his still-sobbing wife out.

People are strange, Jenny thought. It

takes all kinds. This woman wouldn't or couldn't control herself. Others were stoic, not permitting themselves to think of what could have happened. One lady sat quietly apart, hands folded. It was the hardest thing Jenny had ever done not to go to her. Her husband was one of the most seriously burned; he had been caught in the midst of the explosion. It would take plastic surgery to restore his features if he lived, and he might not.

But there was little time to dwell on personalities. The night wore on. Each time it seemed relief was in sight, another patient, or two, or three were brought in. Wearily Jenny continued. By now her motions were automatic, though they continued to be effective. She hadn't even had time to think of Lance, desperately fighting upstairs, along with the other surgeons. She had her own job to do; he had his. Time enough later to relive the night, if they ever wanted to.

By six the next morning, Jenny wanted nothing so much as to fall into bed and sleep for a week. But it was after eight before she looked up from her last patient to see Lance in the doorway. The other nurses had been sent home, and Jenny was just finishing when she heard his step.

Funny how she would know it, no matter how tired she was.

"Come home, Nurse Jenny." It was enough. Suddenly all the night's horror swept over the tired girl. All the agony of the people, the concern, the death, and misery compiled into one, got to her. Wordlessly she reached out to Lance, who picked her up for a moment and held her tightly. What comfort in his strong arms! It was all she could do to hold back the tears.

The first thing she said was irrelevant, but he seemed to understand. "I'm glad they had a uniform I could borrow here." She looked down at the filthy uniform, with its evidence of the horror from the night before. Lance followed her train of thought. If there hadn't been a uniform, it would have been her lace wedding dress that would now be ruined beyond cleaning. Yet even so, he knew it wouldn't have stopped Jenny. When she was needed, she went. It wouldn't have mattered that she had to sacrifice a cherished dress. With growing wonder, he thought, That is one of the reasons I love her so much, her unselfishness.

"I'm so tired." Her words were muffled against his chest, her eyes half closed in sleep as he led her to the car. He gently helped her in; she was asleep before he backed out of the parking lot.

"She's just all in," he told the concerned Matthewsons, who met them at the door. "She worked all night long."

She didn't waken even when he carried her to her own room and Mrs. Matthewson gently removed the soiled uniform, smiling at the lacy party slip underneath, and tucked her in bed. Although there were dark circles of weariness under Dr. Lance's own eyes, he didn't have time for rest.

"Yes, I'll have a cup of that coffee and get back," he told the good old lady. She heaped his plate high with fresh cinnamon rolls and the scrambled eggs Mr. Matthewson had finished stirring while she put Jenny to bed.

"See that she sleeps as long as she wants. I disconnected the phone. I'll call you if I need anything. When she wakes up, ask if she can come back on duty, and tell her I'm all right."

Mrs. Matthewson nodded. Jenny had looked like a little white ghost when Lance brought her home. She needed the rest.

Lance needn't have worried about Jenny not getting enough rest. She slept until six o'clock that night. Waking, she couldn't

213

adjust to the quiet room. How had she gotten here? The last thing she remembered was leaning against Lance in the deserted emergency room. A soft tap at the door brought her upright in bed. Where was Lance?

Mrs. Matthewson came in with a tray. "He went back. He was needed."

Jenny threw back the covers. "Why didn't you call me?"

Mrs. Matthewson shivered in mock fear. "And disobey Dr. Reeves? It would have been 'off with my head' if I had disturbed you!" She was relieved to see Jenny laugh as she headed for the shower. "Hurry, your dinner will be cold!"

It didn't take the girl long. Slipping into a golden housecoat that brought out highlights in the shining chestnut hair, Jenny attacked the food Mrs. Matthewson had brought. There wasn't a scrap left when she spoke again.

"I was starved!"

"You wouldn't have had to tell me. Your plate shows that!"

Jenny threw her arms around the good woman with an impulsive hug. "You know you spoil us, bringing me a tray like this!"

The action startled Mrs. Matthewson. "Land's sakes, child, I didn't do anything!

If you and Dr. Lance can work all night patching folks up, the least I can do is feed you!"

Jenny stared at her. "You're right. It takes all of us, doesn't it? But I'm glad we live here. If I'd been alone, I would have grabbed a sandwich and let it go at that."

"You'll need more than a sandwich to get you through this night," Mrs. Matthewson told her wisely. "There will still be a lot to be done. Dr. Lance told me there were a great many seriously injured people. That roast-beef-and-mashed-potato dinner will stick to your ribs like no sandwich could."

"Jenny, are you awake?" It was Lance, who had suddenly appeared at her door. "I came to get you. They need a special for one of the patients. Are you ready?" His glance took in the empty tray and rested face. "Good! Get your uniform on, and we'll get back." Deep lines were etched in his own face. He hadn't had time to rest. He had managed a sketchy lunch, but he was so tired.

"You come down and eat while she's getting dressed." This time it was Mrs. Matthewson who was giving the orders. "You can't go another night on what I bet you've eaten today!" The doctor in him recognized the wisdom of her words, and meekly he followed her downstairs — if Dr. Reeves could ever be called meek!

Mrs. Matthewson took just a minute to load a plate for him. "Now you sit down there and *eat!*"

"Yes, Mother!" There was a suspicious small-boy twist to his words, but she pretended to ignore it.

"Someone needs to make you take care of yourself. You take care of Jenny, but . . ." She deliberately left the sentence unfinished. Lance only nodded. He was eating as rapidly as he could. While what she said was true, there was a lot to be done yet that night.

The world of private duty. Jenny could have written a book on the subject. It was different from any other type of nursing. For one thing, there was no contact with others except when the doctor checked in. With the new facilities for monitoring critical patients, would private nursing become a lost art? she wondered. A slight moan from the patient's bed interrupted her reverie.

"Nurse, my wife?"

"She's fine," Jenny reassured him. "She just slipped away to get some rest." The patient seemed satisfied and fell into a drugged slumber. Jenny reviewed the case. His wife was the quiet, stoic woman of the night before who had so wrung Jenny's heart. She had a heart condition and wasn't supposed to be excited. No wonder the badly burned man in the bed before her was concerned. And how beautiful their long life together must have been! Each had been more worried over the other than over himself.

Lance and I will be like that, Jenny knew with a flash of perception. We're going to be! What we could have is worth fighting for. Lance seems so much more at ease, so relaxed. When I get back to Stehekin, I'm going to lay my cards out on the table and tell him how I feel. Right now we're too busy. But when we get back to Aunt Lucy's "honeymoon cottage," I don't care if it means giving up every bit of pride I own, I'm going to tell him. Then if he doesn't care . . . He has to, she told herself fiercely, he just has to!

But the world of the hospital was no place for personal thoughts. There was work to be done. Jenny rose to check her patient's pulse and temperature. The softly shaded light in the corner didn't disturb the patient, and she was careful to be as still as possible. Right now he needed all the rest he could get. There was a long struggle ahead, but with his grip on life and his wife to support him, he would come through with flying colors.

These are the real, unsung heroes, Jenny thought. Not the doctors or nurses with all their skill, but the patients who valiantly fight their private battles and still come out smiling. A great humility filled the white-clad figure holding the thermometer. She was glad beyond anything in the world that she was a nurse. If you want to be happy, make others happy first. A motto to live by, a talisman. One that Jenny cherished and lived by.

Chapter 13

April thirtieth. The last day of work in Seattle for Lance and Jenny. A day they had looked forward to. A day to take stock of all that had happened since they came back. But most of all, a day of beginning — for tomorrow they would go back to Stehekin!

Jenny paused in her duties for a quick break. It had been a busy day, but she was filled with happiness. For a moment she thought of the many patients she had helped care for during the short months since she had been back in the hospital. She smiled, thinking of those who had come through the terrible Valentine's Day explosion. Only three had died; the others were either recovered and back to work or still undergoing treatment. There was a special place in her heart for the man she had specialed in those days and for his brave wife. There had been a lot for him to go through, but now he, too, was on the mend. That same smile lingered in Jenny's eyes as she entered his room.

"Hello, there!" Her cheerful voice managed to convey all the wonders of spring. It never failed to comfort the tired and weary patients who were fortunate to have Jenny for a nurse. This day the man in the bed responded with a brightening of his own eyes, while his wife in the chair next to him also smiled.

"Isn't it a glorious day?" There was no mistaking the lilt in Jenny's manner.

"Is it a special day for you, my dear?" the wife asked.

"Very!" Jenny found herself sharing with them just how special it was while she straightened the man's pillows, rearranged some flowers that had come in, and checked his temperature, pulse, and respiration.

"So you see," she concluded, "now it's time for us to go home! I mean, to Stehekin."

"Isn't it going to be hard to live in two such different places? Won't you have torn loyalties? You speak of Stehekin as home, yet you've never spent a whole lot of time there, have you?"

Jenny's eyes glowed. "No," she admitted, with a catch of her breath, "but I love it. Even though I've been so grateful we could be here this winter and spring, something seems to be calling me. Each bird I see reminds me of the birds there, singing in the clean, fresh air. It's the same with all the trees and flowers."

"Then how could you bear to leave it at all?"

Jenny was silent for a long moment, thoughtfully regarding this favorite patient and his wife.

"I guess because I've learned that happiness isn't just being where you'd like to be, or where it is peaceful. Happiness comes from being where you're needed. We are needed more here in the wintertime than in Stehekin. Anyway," she said, blushing, "wherever my husband is —" She broke off.

The wife patted Jenny's hand. "I understand. As long as you are together, you will always be at home." Jenny's eyes met the other woman's in a level look of understanding.

That look stayed with Jenny as she finished her duty shift and hurried home. As usual, Mrs. Matthewson had a snack for her. Lance didn't get off until later. In the meanwhile, Jenny did some packing. They planned to leave early the next morning.

"I'm going to miss you," Mrs. Matthewson told the busy girl. "It will seem strange not to have you come bouncing in."

"You won't be as lonely as you think. You'll have Dr. Scofield to feed, and after cooking for himself these past few months, I'm sure he will appreciate your talents!"

Mrs. Matthewson beamed at the praise. "It worked out real well, didn't it? You not only traded jobs with him, but you're trading houses! It will be nice for us. We need someone else here to fuss over."

It was the nearest Jenny had ever heard either of the Matthewsons come to admitting they weren't entirely self-sufficient.

"Where's my wife?" growled a voice at the door, and Lance came in.

"You sound like Father Bear!" Jenny told him.

Lance abandoned his pose. "How near packed are you, Jenny?"

"Just a few more clothes. Why?"

"How would you like to start tonight? We could stop by Leavenworth for a day or two, if you like, and the drive over the pass would be beautiful this evening."

Longing swept over her. "Oh, could we? I won't take but a few minutes to finish here!" There was no doubt that she was delighted.

Lance put his arm around Mrs. Matthewson's ample shoulders and in a loud stage whisper said, "She gets a date to go riding with her very best fella!" Then he roared as Jenny laughed and turned red.

Mrs. Matthewson's keen eyes noted with satisfaction the joy in just being together that the two before her had learned. "I'll pack you a supper you can eat on the way," she put in practically. "No need for you to stop at some unknown place and maybe get poisoned on the food!" Sure of her own good cooking, she distrusted most restaurants, often viewing them as serving ptomaine platters rather than the good home cooking they advertised.

There was a twinkle in Lance's eyes as he stopped her. "Wait, Mrs. Matthewson. Jenny, I have to come back next week."

"What?" Jenny dropped the sweater she had been folding.

"Just for a couple of days. There's this special patient who came through my last difficult surgery with flying colors. I'd love to be able to check on her. She's doing very well, but a visit would really set her on top of the world. Why don't we take the Matthewsons with us tonight? They can see Stehekin, stay this weekend with Twilight and Jeff, and come back with me next week. You can either come or stay and get the cabin settled in. It's only for a few days."

"How great!" Jenny turned to the woman who had meant so much in her life and in the life of Twilight. "Will you come? You can see Tommy Two and —"

"Hold everything. I'll just run down and ask the Mister." She disappeared down the stairs and in a moment was back with her husband. It didn't take long to convince them, and in a flurry they were off to pack. Seldom had Jenny seen the old couple so excited, and how wonderful of Lance to think of it!

"Don't bring any food," Lance called after Mrs. Matthewson. "Dinner's on me, and you'll like this place!"

Jenny was surprised at her feelings as they drove away from Seattle in the late-afternoon glow. Looking back at the Space Needle etched against the sky, she thought of how in the past few months she had really begun to know Lance. The long walks on the beach. The strolls through the Arboretum. All the many crazy things he had found to do while courting her, as he stubbornly referred to it.

And yet a little depression filled her. These had been drifting days, a growing time. Now they were over forever. Before her lay the necessity of setting things right. Or could they be set right? Was the little boat of marriage she and Lance had so heedlessly embarked on strong enough to weather the storms, or was it leaky? As soon as she and Lance reached the cottage, she was going to get it over with. If his response was negative, then would be time enough to face it. She didn't want his pity, only his love. No, she corrected herself, I want more than just his love. I want his liking, too. I want his friendship.

Friendship. She remembered so well the day that he had told her not to come back as a friend, he wanted a wife. Well, now she had his friendship, in spite of them both. The wife part remained to be seen. In the meantime, she needed to concentrate on the Matthewsons.

Lance was doing some remembering of his own. It was almost a year since he had first come to Stehekin. A bridegroom. What category did he fall into now? There was one thing about it. When they reached Stehekin, things were going to have to be cleared up with Jenny. All these weeks he had held himself under an iron control. Now, with her friendliness, that control was slipping. He had her friendship; he wanted more, so much more!

His heart cried out for the wife she had never yet been except in name. A series of pictures flashed through his mind. Jenny, defying him in the Seattle hospital. Jenny, his bride. Jenny, saying table grace. Jenny, skillfully attending a patient. Jenny, Jenny, Jenny. What would the future bring? His determination to hold her weakened. What if she really does love someone else? Yet in word or deed, all this time, there has never been any apparent interest in anyone or longing for another.

Forcing his thoughts to the present, he called back, "Everything under control back there?"

The Matthewsons smiled at his question. "You bet!"

He could see the older couple were enjoying themselves tremendously, sitting as close to one another as a pair of young lovers. The drive across the pass, as Lance had predicted, was absolutely beautiful. It was light enough in the long evening to see the blossoms of spring gracing the various fruit trees, resembling heaps and billows of pale pink or white whipping cream. The darker green of evergreen trees provided a magnificent background for the more delicately clad pale green willows and cottonwoods.

"The air smells so good!" Mrs. Matthewson said.

Lance and Jenny couldn't help but laugh at the Matthewsons. They were so obviously delighted with everything they saw. They breathed in great gulps of the fresh air pungent with spicy pine aroma. It was their first trip into that part of Washington State and they were enjoying every minute of it. Their first glimpse of Leavenworth confirmed all their expectations. To Lance and Jenny, it was beautiful because of familiarity. To the Matthewsons, it was charming because of its newness. Everywhere they looked there was something else to see.

Lance had made reservations at the same motel they had stayed in during the Christmas holidays. Shortly after their arrival, they were ushered into the same downtown restaurant they had gorged themselves in before. Even the same bubbly, charming waitress waited on them, eyes widening in recognition.

"Aren't you the doctor and one of the nurses who helped out in our hospital a few months ago?"

When they admitted they were she told them, "You'll never know how much we appreciate it. It was my brother in that car accident with you, and all he has talked about since was the special care you took of him. I saw you when I came to the hospital to ask how he was, but I didn't get to meet you then." Her warm gratitude added the crowning touch to the happy evening.

Although at first Mrs. Matthewson eyed the Bavarian food on the menu with distrust, at last she was persuaded to try it.

"If you don't care for it, I'll get you a good old American steak," Lance promised. But happily enough, she and Mr. Matthewson both liked it once it came. Their waitress was outstanding in her devotion to duty, and their apple strudel was piled high with whipped cream. By the time the rollicking entertainment came on, they were full to the brim.

"Don't know when we've had such a good time," Mr. Matthewson said. "Mighty glad you young folks brought us."

"We're glad you came." Lance's voice was quiet but intent. "You'll never know how good it has been to know that when I was called out nights, Jenny was right there safe in your home, or I should say, 'our' home. That's what it is."

Breaking the spell of the evening he reminded them, "It's almost closing time. We'd better go."

Mrs. Matthewson was able to shop to

her heart's content the next day in the little shops, with all their attractive wares. She was like a little girl, picking up one treasure after another, hugging each one to herself, carrying it around until she found another thing she liked better. She was especially fascinated with mugs that had her and Mr. Matthewson's first names on them.

He followed after her, enjoying her absorption, gently reminding her, "Buy what you like, but what are you going to use those things for?"

Good-naturedly she put them back, confessing she would probably never use the trinkets for anything, she was just held by their expert craftsmanship and beauty.

Jenny and Lance bought a beautifully carved cuckoo clock for Don and Ann, after watching and listening to all the varieties, with their colorful figures that marched in and out. They also bought a wrought-metal spray of flowers, delicately painted, for Twilight and Jeff's mantel. It would add just the right touch.

The Matthewsons' first glimpse of Lake Chelan thrilled Jenny. They thought it was just as blue and wonderful as she remembered it, or had it gotten even bluer since she'd been gone? Yet, Lake Washington was blue and deep, too. Perhaps this was special because it was so unexpected, finding such a large lake in such otherwise arid country. Chelan itself was a busy little town, sometimes overlooked in favor of Leavenworth, but clean and pretty in its own right. They enjoyed their dinner and night there immensely, having found a young boy in the restaurant who liked to talk and who gave them a lot of valuable information about the area.

And then it was time. Time to board the *Lady of the Lake*. Time to start the long trip up the lake. Time to stand by the rail and watch the foam stirred up by their passing. After a while, the Matthewsons went inside to watch their progress from the glass windows that afforded a lovely view. It was nippy on the water, but Jenny could hardly be torn from her post. She wanted to see everything. Her eyes were starving for the first glimpse of Stehekin and her sister and all the wild and rugged scenery that lay ahead.

Lance watched her unobtrusively. He was wise enough to know that there were certain times that people needed to be left totally alone. For there was a place — a private place — within every human being that one had to be able to withdraw to at times. Those who had not discovered it were the ones who sometimes couldn't face the challenges of life. They had never learned to accept themselves, and thus they could not cope with the outside world.

So now he sat back, enjoying not only the mountain scenery that was becoming more profuse but also Jenny's profile as she eagerly strained her eyes ahead for that first glimpse of her beloved country. Unlike some, he had no feeling of being shut out. Rather, he shared with her even more that ability to be still and to appreciate.

"There it is!" Her eager cry sent him hurrying to bring the Matthewsons out. Together, the four of them watched the approach to the landing. Dimly, the figures on shore became clearer.

"Twilight! Jeff! Tommy Two!"

Jenny's scream of sheer excitement was lost in her sister's amazed but undignified whoop, "Jenny — the Matthewsons!" The usually self-composed Twilight thrust Tommy Two into Jeff's arms and ran full speed to the very edge of the shore. Only making sure to stay clear of the landing boat, she was on deck almost before it was secured.

"Oh, I'm glad you've come!" she told the Matthewsons. "You can stay with us. Lance and Jenny are crowded for room. Then, too, Dr. Scofield still has some of his gear at their place. How long can you stay?" Her great purple eyes were more brilliant than ever in her happiness.

"So you like the present we brought you?" Lance managed to insert.

She turned on him in an instant, throwing her arms around him and giving him a sisterly kiss. It left him wordless.

"You're blushing," Jenny pointed out demurely. But she wasn't to have the last word after all.

A wicked gleam crept into his eyes. "Are you ready to go out to 'honeymoon cottage'?" he asked innocently.

She was saved from replying by Ann, who managed to get through the crowd surrounding them now that they had managed to finally get ashore.

"Ann!" Her red-haired friend was positively glowing. Married life certainly agreed with her. Jenny said as much.

"That's not all." Ann tossed her head, then lowered her voice. "When will Lance be set up for office hours?"

"Probably tomorrow. Why?"

Ann lowered her eyelids in a vain

attempt to hide the mischief lurking there, which would give her away to Jenny in a minute.

"I just thought I'd let him check me over and confirm something."

"Ann!" Jenny's voice was thrilled. "You're pregnant?"

"I hope so." Ann looked at her friend of so many years square in the eyes. "We don't want to wait to have children. We want them now, while we're young. Don't say anything," she cautioned as Don came forward to welcome Jenny.

Jenny concluded Ann wasn't going to say anything until she was sure. She could also understand how Ann had waited for Lance rather than going to Dr. Scofield, wonderful though he was. Ann would feel disloyal to let anyone other than Lance confirm her happiness. Jenny's heart almost burst with happiness. What wonderful news! Now if only she and Lance . . .

"Come on, Jenny, let's go!" someone shouted.

They were ready to start, every available vehicle packed with luggage. Dr. Scofield had gone on ahead to get the rest of his gear and take it out to Twilight and Jeff's. Their house was so much larger. Then, too, he would be a little freer to come and go his last few days in Stehekin, until fall. He could slip down to the big kitchen and grab a bite before tramping around early, as had become his habit. Stehekin had been good for him. He looked rested, happy. He was ready to go back to Seattle and serve for the summer.

And so, after delivering the delighted Matthewsons and having dinner, Jenny and Lance went back to the "honeymoon cottage" alone. The sun had fallen low in the sky while they had reminisced at dinner. Evening had come, the twilight shadows for which Jenny's sister was named, and the time of day they both loved. But now there was another love of the quiet evening hours.

A ray of sun took aim with a parting shot to light the cottage with a single piercing beam just as they drove to the door. The logs seemed afire for a moment, the windows gleamed gold. The front door stood invitingly open. Dr. Scofield had purposely left it so. What lay beyond that threshold, happiness or heartbreak? Still seated in the car, Lance and Jenny were busy with their own thoughts. Neither had spoken since leaving Twilight and Jeff's.

I don't want to go inside, Jenny thought dully. I wish I could hold back time. The cottage was . . . was glorified in the light.

I wish I could hold this moment forever, and yet there is a waiting in it, a waiting for me to make the first move. Nature painted pictures such as the one before them. Only love could paint a home. Aunt Lucy's cabin wasn't just a cabin. It was a real home . . . or could be.

First Lance stepped out of the car. Then as Jenny started out on the other side, he scooped her up in his strong arms. She could feel his heart beating rapidly and realized this tremulous moment was as hard for him as for her. That realization gave her courage to speak as he carried his bride of so many months across the threshold.

"Lancelot, you are another man from the one who carried me across this threshold last winter."

Another man. The words rang a bell deep inside Lance. He repeated them after her. "Another man? Jenny, did you mean me? That day when you told me you had fallen in love with another man, was it me?"

Jenny couldn't raise her eyes to his for fear of what she might find in them. His voice had been so incredulous she was afraid of his feelings. But she had promised herself not another day would go by before she had been honest with him.

"Yes . . . I wanted to tell you . . ." Her voice faltered and broke.

"Jenny, look at me."

Slowly her long lashes raised, her misty eyes gazed into his. And she found surprise, wonderment, ecstasy. There was nothing in his own look but pure love. Gone was all coldness, all sarcasm.

"And all this time I thought . . ." He choked off the words that would recall the past.

"Me, too." Her voice was small, ashamed.

His arms tightened, holding her as if he would never let her go, and he didn't intend to. "Welcome home, Nurse Jenny. Welcome home, Guinevere . . . beloved." The last word was almost a whisper.

For a moment all that had transpired in the little cottage flashed across Jenny's mind. The truce. The friendship. The coldness. The anger. The worry. And now the realization of her husband's great love. Jenny's heart was in her eyes, eyes that looked up clear and trusting into her man's.

"Lancelot . . . I *am* home."

We hope you have enjoyed this Large Print book. Other Thorndike Press or Chivers Press Large Print books are available at your library or directly from the publishers.

For more information about current and upcoming titles, please call or write, without obligation, to:

Thorndike Press
P.O. Box 159
Thorndike, Maine 04986 USA
Tel. (800) 257-5157

OR

Chivers Press Limited
Windsor Bridge Road
Bath BA2 3AX
England
Tel. (0225) 335336

All our Large Print titles are designed for easy reading, and all our books are made to last.